on Holiday

Look out for other books
by Julian Clary & David Roberts:

The Bolds

The Bolds to the Rescue

THE BOLDS

on Holiday

By Julian Clary

Illustrated by
David Roberts

Andersen Press • London

First published in 2017 by
Andersen Press Limited
20 Vauxhall Bridge Road
London SW1V 2SA
www.andersenpress.co.uk

2 4 6 8 10 9 7 5 3 1

British Library Cataloguing in Publication Data available.

ISBN 978 1 78344 506 6

Printed and bound in Great Britain by
Clays Limited, Bungay, Suffolk, NR35 1ED

For my
husband Ian

JC

For my
husband Chris

DR

Chapter

Have you ever noticed that some people's lives are more exciting than others? Things seem to happen to some people.

They'll be walking along the street, maybe going to post a letter, minding their own business and then something occurs... Maybe they witness a bank robbery or they bump into someone famous from the telly or their trousers fall down. For these people life is action-packed, every day wherever they are, while for you and me – well, we go out, post our letter, come home – and that will be that. Nothing wildly exciting happens at all!

The Bolds are the sort of people to whom things just seem to happen. Quite big, exciting things, through no fault of their own. They don't go looking for adventures, adventures just seem to find them. Maybe this is because they are unusual people . . .

Well, let's not beat about the bush, the Bolds aren't actually people at all. They are, as you may have heard, a family of hyenas living disguised as humans. They have to keep their tails and their animal ways hidden, but they've got rather good at that and, so far, no one has rumbled them.

Now, like all hyenas, the Bolds spend most

of their time laughing, and to cover this fact Mr Bold has got himself a job writing the jokes for Christmas

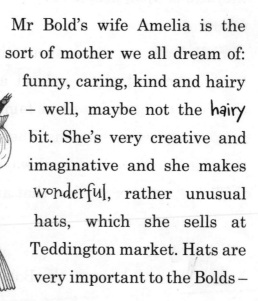

crackers. Consequently he tells jokes quite often. *Too* often, some might say. But he loves his job and it pays the bills and he is very happy.

Mr Bold's wife Amelia is the sort of mother we all dream of: funny, caring, kind and hairy – well, maybe not the hairy bit. She's very creative and imaginative and she makes wonderful, rather unusual hats, which she sells at Teddington market. Hats are very important to the Bolds –

almost as important as jokes – because they're part of their disguise and allow them to live undiscovered in the world amongst humans.

Mr and Mrs Bold live in an ordinary semi-detached house in Teddington with their twins, Bobby and Betty, and another elderly hyena called Uncle Tony, whom they rescued from a safari park. Oh, and let's not forget Miranda, a marmoset monkey, who came with Uncle Tony from the safari park.

They all live at Number 41 Fairfield Road, and their next-door neighbour is Mr Nigel McNumpty (a grizzly bear, as it happens) and they get along very well. So well, in fact, they are all planning to go on a two-week camping holiday together this summer. By the seaside.

The twins are very excited as they've never seen the sea before. Knowing the Bolds as we do, though, it is unlikely to be a nice, restful holiday, is it? Something is bound to happen . . .

Now, the only human who knows about the Bolds' and Mr McNumpty's real identities is the twins' best friend, Minnie. She was understandably shocked when she first heard, but has promised to keep the secret safe and never tell a soul. And so far she has proved true to her word. She spends a lot of time at the Bolds' house, because it is a lot more fun than her own, and her parents have even agreed that she can go on the camping holiday with the Bolds. Everyone is **very** excited.

But before the holidays can begin, school must finish – and on the last day of term Bobby and Betty are having their school Sports Day.

I'm sure it's the same at your school too. At the twins' school they call it a Fun Sports Day but I'm not sure everyone finds Sports Day fun. (I certainly never did and I didn't have a tail hidden in my shorts. I wasn't the sporty type. But enough about me.) Anyway, Betty and Bobby's Sports Day was on a beautiful sunny July afternoon, and Mr and Mrs Bold, Uncle Tony, Miranda and Mr McNumpty came along with all the other parents and relatives to watch and cheer.

Mr Bold parked the little blue Honda in the car park and the excited party made their way onto the playing field carrying a picnic rug and a deckchair for Uncle Tony. A crowd of spectators had already gathered and a few eager parents had been there since early in the morning to get a good spot. (Some people really can get over-competitive on a Sports Day.)

Mrs Bold was wearing a nice floral summer frock and one of her self-made hats: this one was specially designed for the occasion, and featured bunting, water bottles, fruit and several pairs of plimsolls jauntily bobbing up and down on springs. It was a little top-heavy and she needed to hold onto it to stop it toppling over to one side. Uncle Tony was pushing Miranda in her little doll's pushchair and Mr McNumpty was striding along looking very gentlemanly in a pale blue suit and white fedora hat.

Mr Bold could hardly contain his excitement about the proceedings. 'Come on, you BOLDS!' he shouted. 'We are the champ-i-ons!'

'Hush, dear,' said Mrs Bold. 'It's a fun sports day, remember? It's not the winning that matters, it's the taking part. Mrs Millin – the twins' class teacher – says they're all winners at this school.'

'Well, I know, Amelia,' he replied. 'But we both know that's not true. Look at that boy over there,' he said, pointing to a little chap who was busy picking his nose and wiping it on his shirt. 'He's definitely not a winner, and we both know that the twins could easily win every event if only . . .'

'Lower your voice,' hissed Mrs Bold, guessing what he might be about to say.

'If only they didn't have to run on just two legs,' whispered Fred. 'A hyena could outrun a human any day of the week if we were back in Africa using all four legs.'

'I know,' giggled Mrs Bold. 'What fun that would be!'

'As it is we rather struggle waddling about on our hind trotters. Poor Bobby really wasn't looking forward to today. He's sure he'll come last and it's very frustrating for him. That boy in his class, Kyle, has teased him about how slow he is. I'd like to tear a strip off him, I really would. I can feel myself starting to growl just looking at him. Grrrr . . . Grrrr!'

'Now, now, stay calm, old chap,' said Mr McNumpty firmly. 'Coming last is a small price to pay for the life we lead. A lot more civilised than out in the wild, remember. We're happy living as humans and we want it to stay that way.'

'Quite so,' said Mrs Bold, licking her lips and waving to Millie's father, who was setting out a picnic of lovely-looking ham and cold sausages he'd no doubt brought from his butcher's shop in Teddington High Street. 'I just hope Bobby's remembered to tuck his tail into his shorts properly.'

'I think it's time for a joke,' said Mr Bold.

Did you hear about the race between the lettuce and the tomato?

The lettuce got a 'head' and the tomato was trying to 'ketchup'!

Just then Mrs Millin approached the Bolds, smiling brightly and holding a clipboard.

'Good afternoon everyone, how lovely to see you. What a, er, clever hat, Mrs Bold. One of your own, I imagine?'

'Yes, Mrs Millin,' said Amelia, giving an unnecessary curtsey.

'Splendid! How creative you are.'

Mrs Millin raised her clipboard and produced a pen. 'Now then. Can I put you both down for the Parents' Race? It's a lot of fun!'

'Oh, we like fun,' said Mrs Bold, nodding. 'Count us in!'

'Jolly good,' said Mrs Millin, marking their names on her clipboard. 'Best of luck.'

Just then there was an announcement on the loudspeaker: 'Ladies and Gentlemen, Boys and Girls, the first race of the afternoon is the Three-Legged Race. Starting in two minutes!'

'Ooh, Bobby and Betty are in this,' said Uncle Tony. 'Let's get a place at the front so we can cheer them on.'

Chapter

The Bolds' party found a nice spot to settle down in, with an excellent view of the athletics track and next to George, Minnie's father, who was tucking into a juicy pork pie.

'What a lovely spread!' declared Mr Bold, his mouth watering as he looked at the plate piled high with sausages. 'And is that a birthday cake I can see?'

'Afternoon, all,' said George. 'Yes. It's Minnie's birthday today. I thought a picnic might cheer her up.'

'Cheer her up? Oh, what is the matter?' asked Mrs Bold, concerned.

George sighed. 'Minnie badly wanted a puppy for her present this year. But we can't have all that mess and trouble.'

'Mess? Trouble?' said Mr Bold, feeling rather insulted. 'Why, animals are no more trouble than humans. In fact, in my experience, animals can be a good deal cleaner and easier.'

'Now then, Fred,' said Mrs Bold, worrying that her husband would say too much. 'The race is about to start.'

'It's not just that,' added George, trying to make his peace with Mr Bold. 'I'm afraid I'm allergic to animal hair. Makes me – a-chooo! – sneeze. A-chooo! A-choo! Do excuse me! There must be some animals around here,

17

but I can't see any.'

Mr and Mrs Bold glanced at each other and stifled a giggle.

'Bless you!' said Mrs Bold.

Everyone settled themselves on the grass, ready for the first race to begin. Five pairs of eyes looked hungrily at the picnic but George didn't seem to notice.

'What racey Minnie in?' squeaked Miranda.

'The Hula Hooping!' said her father, before sneezing some more.

'That's right,' said Mr McNumpty. 'Seen her practising in the garden with Betty. Betty didn't seem to have the waist for it, but Minnie could hula several hoops at once. An excellent hula hooper!'

There was a shrill whistle and the three-legged racers were off. There were ten pairs of children, one leg each tied together, doing their best to race along the track with varying degrees of success. The crowd cheered and craned their necks to see.

'Come on, Bobby and Betty!' shouted Mr Bold. 'You can do it!'

'Where are they? I can't see them,' frowned Mrs Bold.

'Er, at the back,' said Mr Bold.

It was true. Right from the start it was clear the twins were hopeless at three-legged racing. The truth was, it is difficult enough for hyenas to walk on their two hind legs, without one of those legs being tied to someone else's. This made walking, let alone running, doubly

tricky, and it didn't help that the twins were helpless with laughter.

'Oh, sis,' said Bobby, gasping for air between shrieks of laughter, 'I was dreading this but it's actually so much fun!'

'I know, Bobs,' wheezed Betty. 'The others are so far ahead I can hardly see them! We're definitely going to lose. It couldn't be funnier.'

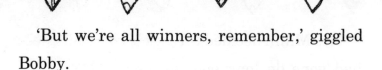

'But we're all winners, remember,' giggled Bobby.

'Bob-by! Bet-ty! Come on, you can do it!' cried the Bolds, with not much conviction. But it wasn't happening. As the winning pair crossed the finish line, the twins had barely started. The eyes of the crowd turned to the young hyenas who were making an awful lot of noise whooping, giggling and slapping each other on the shoulders.

'They're having fun, aren't they?' said a man behind the Bolds. 'That's the main thing.'

The race was now finished – apart from the twins, who, to the delight of the crowd, had toppled over and were lying on their backs, their legs waving in the air as they gave in completely to the hilarity of the situation. The crowd burst into spontaneous applause.

Mrs Millin decided the whole sorry business had gone on long enough, and marched onto the track to help the twins up and untie their legs.

'Thank you, Bobby. Thank you, Betty,' she said briskly. 'Up you get, please. We don't want our Sports Day turning into a shambles now, do we? Off you go, children.' There was a final cheer of appreciation from the crowd.

George turned to Mr and Mrs Bold. 'What a hilarious pair!' he said, smiling. 'No wonder our Minnie likes to spend so much time with them.'

'Mmm!' agreed Mrs Bold, nodding, but keeping her mouth firmly clamped shut. As in fact did Mr Bold, Uncle Tony, Mr McNumpty and Miranda . . .

George then glanced down at his picnic and was surprised to see the plate of sausages strangely depleted. In fact, there were only three left. 'Where have all my sausages gone?' he asked, scratching his head.

Mr Bold swallowed quickly. 'Oh, er, pigeons, I expect,' he said. 'Such a menace these days. Delicious sausages, though. I expect. The pigeons said. If they could speak. Which they can't.'

George eyed Fred suspiciously, then sneezed again. 'A-choo!'

Mr Bold decided to tell a joke to divert everyone's attention from the missing sausages.

How do you make a sausage roll?

Push it downhill!

Everyone laughed, and George thought he saw a piece of chewed-up sausage in Uncle Tony's open mouth, but he couldn't be sure. *And what exceedingly large teeth he has*, he thought, *come to think of it . . .*

Suddenly there was a welcome distraction.

'It's Hula Hooping time!' boomed the announcement. 'The winner will be the child who can keep his or her hoop spinning for the longest.'

'It's Minnie's event!' cried Mrs Bold, and all attention turned to the field – although George thought it wise to move the birthday cake as far away from the Bolds as possible.

A line of children took their places, each

holding a hoop around their waist, ready to begin. Minnie was near the end, smiling nervously.

The whistle blew and the children began hula hooping, encouraged by the crowd of parents and friends. One or two dropped out almost at once, but five – including Minnie – hula hooped with confidence, holding their arms wide while their hips swivelled and the hoops spun about, up and down, round and round.

'Go, Minnie!' George shouted between sniffs and sneezes, and the Bolds all hollered and chanted Minnie's name. Eventually there were just two competitors left: Minnie and a taller girl called Jasmine.

'These two are brilliant!' came the announcement.

The crowd were on their feet, cheering.

'Minnie!'

'Jasmine!'

'MINNIE, MINNIE!'

'JASMINE! JASMINE!' they shouted.

'These two are never going to stop!' said the commentator, and it seemed to be true.

Both girls were getting red in the face. On and on they went, beads of sweat running down their cheeks.

'Incredible!' said the announcer.

Finally Jasmine had to stop, clutching her side as if she had a stitch.

'Minnie is the winner!'

Everyone cheered, and Mr Bold patted George on the back to congratulate him.

'I'm so pleased for Minnie,' sighed Mrs Bold. 'And on her birthday too!'

There were only two events left now: High Jump (Betty was going to have a go) and Long Jump (Bobby was in this). Then came the grand finale of the day, the Parents' Race.

29

Mr and Mrs Bold knew that their children weren't going to win anything. There were really no sporting events where being a hyena was an advantage. Walking (or running or jumping) on two feet when you really should be using four more or less ruined your chances, to be honest.

So in the High Jump, as you might have guessed, Betty didn't triumph. She jumped with all her hyena might, but only managed a few centimetres. Bobby watched his sister and thought how unfair it was. Although it was true they were having fun, wouldn't it be nice to win something, like Minnie, and collect a winner's medal at the prize-giving?

In Bobby's Long Jump event each competitor had three goes. After his first two attempts Bobby was at the bottom of the results board, way behind the others and

simply miles behind the leader – that rather nasty boy called Kyle who was clearly feeling very cocky and sure of himself.

'You've got no chance, Boldie,' he sneered at Bobby. 'I'm the winner and you might as well go home now.' And Kyle gave Bobby a vicious shove, which knocked him over, onto all fours.

As he got up and brushed the dirt and grass off his legs, Bobby suddenly had an idea. A rather good idea, he thought . . . a rather Bold idea.

Preparing for his final jump, Bobby stood at the start line and heard Kyle behind him quietly chanting under his breath, 'Loser! Loser!'

Right. That decided it. Bobby took several deep breaths and lowered his head. Suddenly a look of animal determination came across him and he began his run.

But this time, instead of the awkward hind-leg run he usually did, Bobby dropped down onto his front legs and ran like the hyena he really was. Suddenly his speed was tripled – he flew along like a greyhound, bounding faster by the second, his long hyena tongue hanging out the side of his mouth. As he reached the

end of the runway his hind legs propelled
him up, up up in the sky. His front paws
paddled the air and his whole body wriggled
and strained, rather like a fish leaping
out of the water. The spectators
were suddenly stunned
into silence.

Bobby seemed to fly through the air for
ages until, finally, he landed, several metres
ahead of the mark that showed where Kyle,

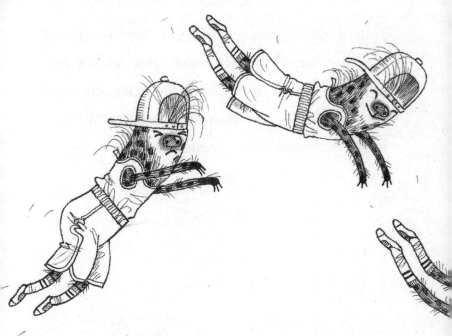

the current leader, had jumped
to. There was a collective gasp from
the crowd, then an eruption of amazed
cheering and applause. Bobby hoisted himself
up onto his back legs again, tucked his tongue
back in his mouth and smiled with satisfaction.
He'd won! And very convincingly indeed.

'But you can't— It isn't fair!' said a furious
Kyle, running up to Mrs Millin to complain.

Mrs Millin shrugged. 'Well, there's nothing in the rules about not using your hands and legs,' she said. 'Bobby is the winner, fair and square, I'm afraid. Don't be such a bad loser, Kyle! Remember, we're all winners here.'

Mr and Mrs Bold beamed with pride and giggled to themselves. 'He really shouldn't have . . . but I'm glad he did!' said Mrs Bold to her husband.

'You can take the hyena out of the wild, but you can't take the wild out of the hyena,' whispered Fred in a rare display of wisdom. 'Well done, my son!'

For his last jump, Kyle attempted to do the same as Bobby, but only succeeded in rolling head over heels before he even got to jump. He stomped off looking furious.

'What a win for young Bobby Bold!' boomed the voice over the loudspeakers. 'And now, our most fun event of all, the Parents' Race – would all the competitors please make their way to the starting line.'

Chapter

'Ooh, the Parents' Race,' said Mr Bold. 'That's us. Come on, dear. Are you joining in, George?'

'Er. Well. I wish I could, but I can't stop this sneezing. Such a nuisance. And what about the birthday cake?' said George, looking up in the sky in case any hungry pigeons were circling.

'We'll guard it for you, won't we, Tony?' said Mr McNumpty.

'Oh yes,' nodded Tony, eyeing the tasty

Victoria sponge hungrily. 'We'll cake – I mean, take very good care of it . . .'

'That's very kind,' said George, getting up and flexing his legs in preparation for the race.

'Tony,' said Mrs Bold in a warning tone, leaning over to whisper in his ear. 'Behave. Don't touch a crumb, do you hear? Bobby's nearly given the game away and I don't want you doing the same.'

Mr and Mrs Bold set off for the start line with George. 'I'm not sure how easy it is going to be to run in this hat,' pondered Amelia.

'Take it off, then,' suggested George.

'Well, I can't really because . . . well . . .' What she wanted to say was, I can't because it's hiding my hyena ears. But of course she

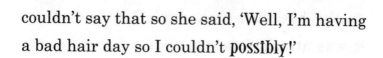

couldn't say that so she said, 'Well, I'm having a bad hair day so I couldn't possibly!'

'Ah, yes,' said George, looking far from convinced. 'A-choo!'

So, how well do you think Mr and Mrs Bold did in the Parents' Race? Do you think they came in the top three? No, of course not! Do you think something maybe went wrong?

Yes, that's right. How clever you are. The Bolds couldn't run very well at the best of times, for reasons we've already discussed. But the main problem in this race was Mrs Bold's hat. As she ran, it toppled over. Mr Bold tried to catch it for her, but only succeeded in punching it up in the air. One of the plimsolls

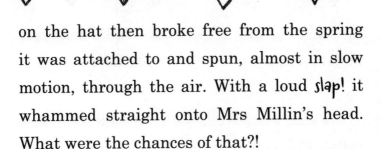

on the hat then broke free from the spring it was attached to and spun, almost in slow motion, through the air. With a loud slap! it whammed straight onto Mrs Millin's head. What were the chances of that?!

Mrs Millin wasn't best pleased and she blew her whistle very loudly to disqualify the Bolds. But they didn't mind. They were laughing so much they couldn't have continued anyway.

'Oh dear,' said Mrs Bold. 'We're not supposed to be drawing attention

to ourselves and here we are with everyone looking at us.'

So, who won? Well, it was actually Minnie's father George. As soon as he was away from Mr and Mrs Bold his sneezing seemed to stop. He'd never won a race before but I suspect he was hurrying to get back and make sure his cake hadn't been eaten.

Despite severe temptation, Mr McNumpty and Uncle Tony had managed to resist eating the birthday cake – although the ham sandwiches and crisps had all mysteriously vanished – so everyone, including Bobby and Betty and Minnie, enjoyed a slice each after singing a hearty chorus of 'Happy Birthday'.

'Are you having a nice day?' Betty asked her best friend.

'Yes, thank you,' answered Minnie politely.

But Betty could tell something was wrong.
'You won the Hula Hooping competition,'
she reminded Minnie. 'That's
really cool.'

'Mmmm.'

'What's the matter?'

'I've had some lovely presents, and it's great to be a winner. But I didn't get the one thing I really wanted.'

'That's a shame. What were you hoping for?'

'A puppy,' said Minnie, tears welling in her eyes. 'I really, really wanted my own little puppy. You know how much I love animals,' and she gave Betty a knowing look. 'But Dad's allergic to dog hair and that was that.'

'Ah,' said Betty sympathetically, putting her arm round her best friend.

Apart from Minnie's disappointment, everyone agreed the Sports Day had been a great success. The Bolds packed away the blankets, picnic things and what remained

of Mrs Bold's hat and began their walk back to the Honda. Bobby was lagging behind admiring his medal when suddenly that awful Kyle jumped out from behind a parked car and blocked his path.

'Oi! Give me that medal, you!' he hissed.

Bobby looked anxiously around for his parents but they were a long way ahead of him. 'But it's my medal!' he said, reasonably. 'I won. You lost. Now let me past, please, Kyle.'

'Give it to me or I'll punch your big nose,' sneered Kyle, moving even closer to Bobby, and showing him a clenched fist. 'I'll count to three. One . . . two . . .'

Kyle raised his fist high in the air, but Bobby's animal instinct took over and he turned to face Kyle, this time wrinkling his nose and baring his teeth. Kyle took one look at the now ferocious Bobby, screamed and ran in the other direction for all

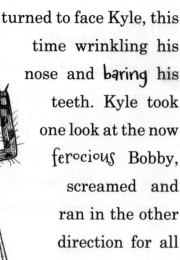

he was worth. Bobby resisted the temptation to run after his prey and sink his teeth into his puffy, pink flesh. Instead he ran as quickly as he could to catch up with his family – this time on his two back legs.

But hyenas aren't as steady on two legs as you or I, and Bobby was very shaken up by what had just happened. He was so cross, he wasn't really looking where he was going – and that's why he didn't see the rabbit hole in the ground until it was too late.

Mr and Mrs Bold and the others heard the commotion and turned round just in time to see Bobby fall to the ground, clutching his left ankle and screaming.

'What's the matter, son?' asked Mr Bold, crouching down next to him.

'My leg! Ooh, ow! It hurts!'

'Oh dear, poor Bobby,' said Mr Bold. 'Let me see.' He gently peeled down Bobby's sock and everyone peered at his rather hairy ankle.

Bobby was moaning with pain. 'Kyle tried to . . . take my medal. I wasn't going to let that happen!' He winced.

'That's swelling up badly,' said George gravely. 'Done yourself a nasty injury.'

Bobby tried to get up but the pain was clearly too much. He began to whimper. 'I – can't – walk on it,' he moaned.

'I'll carry you,' said Mr Bold, picking Bobby up and popping him over his shoulder in a fireman's lift.

'Better take the poor lad to hospital,' said George. 'He'll need an X-ray, that's for sure. A-choo!'

Chapter

Now why do you think it would be a problem for Bobby, or any of the Bolds for that matter, to go to the hospital for an X-ray?

That's right. Because they're animals, not humans, that's why. And the shape of their leg bones is not the same as ours. A doctor would be very suspicious. Heads would be scratched, consultants would be called, and before long the truth would emerge and the Bolds' secret life in Teddington would be in ruins.

'I've always worried something like this might happen one day,' said Mrs Bold once they were safely home at 41 Fairfield Road. Bobby was lying on a pile of cushions on the sofa and Betty was holding a packet of frozen peas on his injured ankle. 'Whatever shall we do? He needs some medical help, Fred, but there's no way a doctor will ever believe he's human once he's been X-rayed and examined thoroughly.'

'Er, don't panic,' said Mr Bold, pacing up and down. 'I'll think of something.' But for Mr Bold the best solution to any problem was always to tell a joke.

Doctor, Doctor, I keep thinking I'm a nit.

Will you please get out of my hair!

Everyone laughed, despite the seriousness of the situation so this encouraged Mr Bold to try another . . .

Doctor, Doctor, I keep thinking I'm a frog.

What's wrong with that?

I'm worried I'm going to croak it.

There was more hyena cackling at this one. But Mr McNumpty stopped laughing first and, frowning, he pointed out that this was getting them nowhere.

'Just one more, please!' pleaded Bobby. 'It doesn't hurt so much when I laugh.'

'Take mind off pain,' Miranda said.

'OK. One last Doctor, Doctor joke. Now let me think . . .' pondered Mr Bold. 'Ah. Got it . . . !

Doctor, Doctor, I keep thinking I'm a dog.

Sit!

The laughter was interrupted again by Mr McNumpty. 'That's it! That's the answer!' he said.

'What is?' asked Uncle Tony.

'Pretend Bobby's a dog. Dogs and hyenas have very similar-shaped bones, don't they?'

'True. But how does that help?' asked Mrs Bold.

'A vet,' Mr McNumpty said simply. 'We'll pretend Bobby is a dog and take him to a vet, not a doctor. The vet can do an X-ray and find out what the problem is.'

There was silence while everyone considered this new option.

Bobby spoke first. 'You mean, take off all my clothes and wear a collar and lead?'

'Yes, that's right,' said Mr McNumpty.

'Would I have to bark and do doggy things?'

'Yup.'

'Wee against lampposts?'

'Er, if you like.'

'Eat my food from a bowl and bury bones in the garden?'

Mrs Bold looked at Bobby sadly. 'I'm sorry, but it may be the only way . . .'

'But I LOVE the idea!' enthused Bobby. 'I could roll around in mud, chew things, rub my bottom on the furniture!'

'Um, steady on now,' said Mrs Bold, looking at her nice new sofa.

'Can I be a dog too, then?' asked Betty.

'No, dear,' said her mother. 'I think one dog will be quite enough.' She was remembering a time, not so long ago, when the house had been full of lots of animals the Bolds had rescued, and much as she missed them, she was rather enjoying having everything a bit more civilised again.

'Brilliant idea. Well done, Nigel!' exclaimed Mr Bold, shaking Mr McNumpty by the paw. 'Now where is the nearest vet's?'

'There's one on the high street,' said Uncle Tony. 'Just next to the ice-cream shop.'

But before he was ready for an appointment there were a few things Bobby had to be taught.

It probably seems strange to you that Bobby, who was really a hyena but who had been pretending to be a human being all of his life, now had to learn to stop acting like a human and behave as an animal. Yes, it is strange, I quite agree. But don't blame me, I'm just telling you the story as I heard it. And if you think this all a bit weird and wonderful, just read on and see what happens in the rest of this book. You ain't heard nothing yet.

Later that afternoon Mr McNumpty popped out to the pet shop and returned with a nice red collar and lead; then Bobby took his clothes off and got down on all fours – although his back left leg was injured, so he had to hop a bit.

'Ah! The joy of letting my tail swish about wherever it wants to is bliss!' sighed Bobby.

'Good,' said Mr Bold. 'But listen. You mustn't speak any more. Not at all, do you understand?'

'Yes,' said Bobby.

'No!' said Mr Bold. 'Don't speak! You're supposed to be a dog. You can only woof, remember. Animals don't talk, or at least humans don't think they do.'

'Got it,' nodded Bobby.

'No, you haven't got it at all,' sighed Mrs Bold. 'Go "woof".'

'Woof!' barked Bobby. 'Is that right?'

58

This was going to take a while, Mr and Mrs Bold agreed.

'How about a muzzle?' suggested Betty, rather unkindly.

'No, please, don't make me wear a muzzle. Everyone will think I'm a dangerous dog if I wear one of those.'

'Well, that's better than a talking dog, I'd have thought,' sniffed Betty.

Bobby sighed. 'Woof, woof,' he said.

'That's better. Now wag your tail in a friendly way,' instructed Mrs Bold. This, Bobby could do with no trouble whatsoever. Stopping his tail from wagging whenever he was happy was something he'd always found very difficult. (In fact, it had to be gaffer-taped to his waist under his trousers all day to prevent suspicious movement below the waist.)

'He ought to have a new name,' suggested Uncle Tony. 'That will remind him he's a dog.'

'I don't need a new name!' cried a bewildered Bobby. 'A dog can be called Bobby, surely?'

'Hush now, bad dog!' said Betty, wagging her finger at her brother.

Bobby gave a little growl.

'Tony is quite right,' said Mr Bold. 'A new name to go with your new life as a dog.'

Bobby wasn't sure he liked this idea.

'Don't worry, dear,' said Mrs Bold, stroking him gently. 'It's only for a little while, so we can get your leg fixed.'

'So what shall we call our new pet?' asked Mr Bold.

'Caesar!' said Mr McNumpty.

'Pork chop!' said Uncle Tony.

'Dude!' said Miranda.

'Handsome!' said Mrs Bold.

'Scruff!' said Mr Bold.

'Susan!' said Betty.

Everyone laughed. Apart from Bobby. He was trying his best not to speak, but in the end he couldn't contain himself.

'I think I should choose my own name!' he cried.

'Stop talking! Bad dog!' scolded Betty.

'Stop talking yourself,' said Bobby, who was in a bit of a bad mood because of the pain in his ankle. 'Or I'll bite you!'

'Mu-m!' shrieked Betty. 'Susan threatened to bite me!'

'Now, now,' said Mrs Bold. 'His name isn't Susan, is it? It's your fault for teasing him. Let's all calm down.'

Mr Bold decided it was time to cheer everyone up with another joke.

What do dogs eat
at the movies?

Pupcorn!

After some discussion it was
decided that Bobby could choose his
own name – it seemed only fair. So without
a moment's hesitation, Bobby announced the
new name he wanted.

'Are you sure the novelty won't wear off
after a while?' asked Mrs Bold when she had
finished laughing.

Bobby shook his head. He had chosen his name for a reason. It was to be a very appropriate name, he decided, smiling to himself. And it was going to be fun!

What do dogs do quite often? While sitting by the fire, maybe? Or after a large meal perhaps? Well, no, it's not only dogs – often humans do it too. But they always try to deny it. Or blame it on the dog. Yes, that's right. They trump, and that was something Bobby had been told off for quite often. Sometimes he did noisy ones, on other occasions they were quiet but deadly . . . Now he was a dog he would do them to his heart's content.

Mr Bold dialled the number for the vet and made an appointment for the next morning.

'And what is the name of your dog?' asked the vet's receptionist.

Chapter

The next morning, Mr and Mrs Bold and Betty set off to the vet's with 'Trumpy', who hopped along quite well on his three good legs. Betty insisted on holding his lead and saying 'Heel!' a lot. Trumpy was thrilled to do his 'business' by a tree while everyone averted their eyes. Betty giggled as her father picked it up with a poo bag and put it safely in a bin.

At the vet's there were quite a few animals in the waiting room with their owners. Several dogs of various sizes and ages wagged their tails at Trumpy and strained on their leads to get a better sniff of him. There were also quite a few cats in travel cages and a rabbit in a cardboard box. You couldn't see it was a rabbit, but the Bolds' noses knew the truth and it smelled delicious.

A big, fluffy cat with very intense green eyes and an expensive diamond collar sat on a lady's lap and hissed menacingly at Trumpy. 'Now, Maureen,' said the cat's owner. 'Be nice.'

Trumpy thought it best to avoid eye contact and shrank back under a chair to avoid provoking Maureen.

Then a lively Labrador puppy came in and bounded up to Trumpy wanting to play.

'Is your dog friendly?' asked the puppy's owner. 'Poppy is only young and can be a bit boisterous.'

'Yes, he's very friendly,' said Mrs Bold.
Meanwhile Poppy got a grip on Trumpy's nose
with her needle-sharp teeth and pulled with
surprising strength.

'Ouch! Get off!' said Bobby involuntarily. Suddenly all the other pet owners and most of the pets looked with amazement at Trumpy. Had that dog just spoken? To cover himself, Bobby then made a few similar-sounding doggy noises. 'Er, groff! Grrroff!'

'Oh my goodness, I actually thought your dog just said "Get off!",' said Poppy's owner, eyes wide with amazement.

'Ha ha!' said Mrs Bold. 'He does make some funny noises. Always, er, g-roffing instead of woofing, aren't you, Trumpy?'

Luckily Poppy had stopped biting and was looking at Bobby with her head on one side, a little confused.

'Bad dog, Trumpy!' said Betty, which Bobby thought was a little uncalled for.

To distract everyone from looking at Bobby, Mr Bold thought it wise to tell a few jokes to the people in the waiting room:

This had the desired effect and soon everyone was so busy laughing, Trumpy's 'talking' was quickly forgotten.

Eventually it was the Bolds' turn to see the vet – a Mr Fleabag.

'What do we have here?' he said, looking down at Bobby. 'He's an ugly little fella, isn't he? Is he as daft as he looks?'

'Not at all. He's very loving and intelligent,' said Mrs Bold, bristling with indignation.

Mr Fleabag shrugged. 'Oh yes. I'm sure he's got a great personality. He'd need to have, looking as scruffy as that.' He laughed.

Scruffy? Mrs Bold was furious and was ready to give the vet a piece of her mind but Mr Bold nudged her. There was no point giving the game away. They needed the vet's help.

'So. Got a poorly leg, has he?' continued the vet, seeing how cross Mrs Bold was starting to look. He picked Bobby up and plonked him on the examination table. 'Haven't seen a dog like this before. A crossbreed, is he?'

'No, he's very happy,' said Mr Bold.

'Something frightful got over the fence, that's for sure,' said Mr Fleabag, shaking his head. He glanced at Bobby's private parts. 'We ought to take those off as well, while he's here. One dog like this in the world is quite enough. Who knows what any pups of his might look like!' He laughed again and tweaked Bobby's ears.

Betty sniggered and Bobby curled his lip.

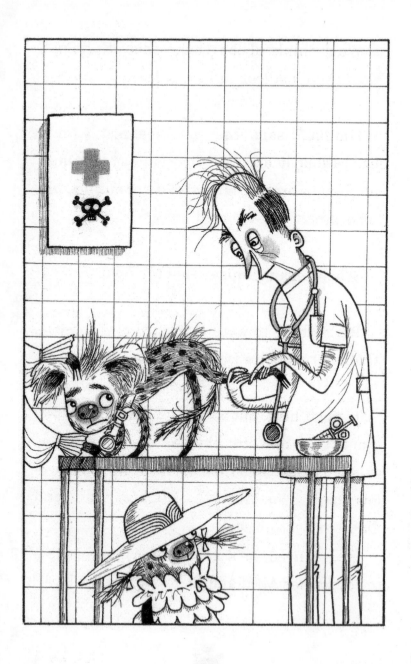

'We'll think about that,' said Mrs Bold. 'Could you just look at his leg for now, please?'

'Hmmm,' said the vet, feeling Bobby's leg, pulling it and twisting it. 'I don't think anything is broken, but we'd better do an X-ray to be sure.'

Bobby began to quiver.

'It's nothing to worry about, Bob— I mean, Trumpy,' said Mrs Bold.

'It won't hurt, but we'll need to anaesthetise him to keep him still, then lie him on his side,' said Mr Fleabag. 'He'll have to stay here a few hours . . .'

'Oh, no need, he'll keep still if you ask him to,' explained Mrs Bold.

'Really?' asked Mr Fleabag.

'Oh yes. He's a very clever dog. Watch this. Which side would you like him to lie on?'

'Right,' said Mr Fleabag. 'But I really don't think—'

'Lie on your right side and play dead, Trumpy, there's a good dog,' said Mrs Bold.

Bobby at once did as he was told, lying flat out on his right side, not moving a muscle, eyes firmly shut.

'Remarkable!' said the vet, scratching his head. 'Will he stay like that?'

'Oh yes,' said Mrs Bold. 'Won't you, Trumpy?'

Bobby nodded.

'I've never seen a dog like it!' exclaimed Mr Fleabag. 'He might be scruffy but he's one of the most intelligent creatures I've ever come across.'

Mrs Bold looked very proud and Bobby gave Betty a knowing wink.

After the X-ray had been taken, Mr Fleabag looked at the results. 'Hmmm,' he said. 'Good. It doesn't seem to be anything serious.'

Bobby's leg wasn't broken, fortunately, so there was no need to put a plaster cast on. But it was badly sprained, and needed to be bandaged.

'He'll need to rest it for at least forty-eight hours,' explained the vet. 'No running about. Just short, slow walks on a lead. We'll give you a crate to keep him in. And because he won't be getting much exercise, cut down on his food. About half of what he usually gets.'

Bobby was aghast and let out a groan.

'All the more for me,' said Betty primly.

'You don't eat dog food, do you, young lady?' laughed Mr Fleabag.

'Just joking,' said Betty awkwardly.

Mr Bold jumped in with a joke:

What do you get
if you cross a dog
with a calculator?

A dog you can
count on!

Mr Fleabag ignored him. 'If he's not showing
any improvement, or if he keeps limping, bring
him back in to me, and I'll have another look.'

'Will we still be able to go on holiday next
week?' asked Mrs Bold anxiously.

'I don't see why not. A bit of sea air will do
him good.'

The Bolds all thanked the vet, and Bobby was put back down on the floor, where he sniffed at his bandaged leg.

'And to stop him biting his bandage, he'll need one of these,' added Mr Fleabag, reaching for a big, pink plastic cone-shaped contraption which he fixed round Bobby's neck. 'It's called an Elizabethan collar. He won't like it, but it's for the best.'

The other Bolds couldn't help but laugh. 'Looks like a lampshade!' shrieked Betty.

'Keep it on day and night,' recommended the vet.

Bobby was not happy. He'd been called 'ugly', told he ought to have his 'bits' cut off, that he was going to be half starved and kept in a crate – and now this!

'And when he's better, I do recommend that he has the snip. You'd never find homes for any pups that look like him,' laughed the vet.

Bobby had just about had enough of Mr Fleabag's insults. He concentrated for a moment, then let out a big, noisy wet trump.

Chapter

It didn't take long for Bobby's leg to start feeling better. A few days' rest, as the vet had said, but without needing to be shut in the crate (which was left in the garden, unused), and he was almost back to normal, although he still limped a bit. It was definitely easier for him to stay on all fours, though. His injured leg was still weak, and when he tried to stand

on two legs like a human being it was very painful. So it was decided Bobby would stay as Trumpy for the two weeks the Bolds were on holiday.

Bobby was quite pleased about this. Now that his leg was starting to feel better, being a dog was good fun. Minnie, who so much wanted a dog of her own, liked to take him out for walks in the park with Betty. Betty thought it was very funny to lead her twin brother around on a lead, make him sit before they crossed the road and tell him off when he was a 'bad dog'. Although he could hear and understand everything said to him, Bobby, as Trumpy, just pretended he couldn't.

'Don't roll in the mud, Trumpy,' said Minnie as they approached a big puddle.

What do you think Trumpy did? Yes, of course. Splat! It was lovely. He also loved chasing and play-fighting all the dogs they met, sniffing, barking and eating tasty morsels left in bins. He was having a lovely time.

Finally the day of departure to Cornwall arrived. Everyone got up early (Minnie had stayed the night) and all eight of them – Mr and Mrs Bold, Uncle Tony, Mr McNumpty, Betty and Bobby, Minnie and Miranda – piled into the blue Honda. It was crammed with luggage and camping equipment. Even more stuff was heaped high on the roof rack. As the car was so full, Miranda, being a monkey, decided she'd be quite happy travelling on the roof.

'Sure you won't fall off?' asked Uncle Tony, concerned.

'Me monkey, me no fall off!' squealed Miranda, poking her head out from under the tarpaulin.

'All aboard?!' asked Mr Bold. 'Seat belts on, everyone.'

It was a very long drive to Cornwall, and after the initial excitement of setting off on their first holiday together, and a rather dreary game of I Spy – 'I spy with my little eye something beginning with R.' 'Road?' 'Correct.' 'S.' 'Sky?' 'Correct.' 'M.' 'Motorway?' 'Correct.' 'C.' 'Clouds?' 'Correct.' 'C.' 'Cars?' 'Correct.' And so on – boredom was beginning to set in.

Any ideas what Mr Bold did to amuse everyone for the next five hours? Yes, that's right. He told jokes, of course. Hundreds of them. I'll pass on a few for you now. Whether these are the 'best' or the 'worst', is up to you. But I can't tell you them all, or there wouldn't be room for the rest of the story. And this tale

has barely started. It does get most exciting, and that's because the Bolds are one of those families that exciting things happen to, remember? But I was going to tell you some of Mr Bold's seaside jokes, wasn't I? Stand by.

What kind of noise annoys an oyster?

A noisy noise annoys an oyster!

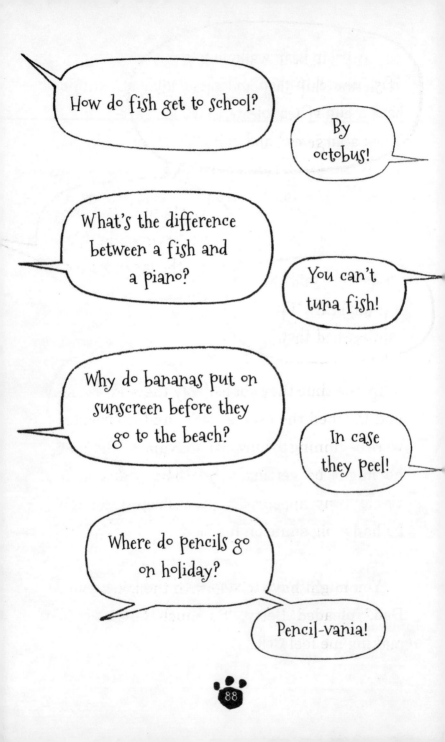

A polar bear walks into a fish and chip shop and says, "I'll have a cup of tea, please, and . . . . . a large cod and chips."

"Certainly," says the girl serving him. "But why the large pause?"

"I dunno," said the polar bear. "I've always had those."

By the time they got halfway there everyone had laughed themselves silly, and their sides were beginning to hurt. Mr McNumpty thought he might be getting a headache – and poor Uncle Tony appeared to be asleep, although he had a big smile on his face.

'You might have to stop with the jokes soon, Dad,' pleaded Betty. 'So much laughing is making me feel sick.'

'We don't want any mess in the back of the car, dear,' said Mrs Bold. 'Perhaps we'd better have a rest from your jokes.'

'Just one more for luck, then,' said Fred.

What time should you go to the dentist?

Tooth-hurty!

The rest of the journey was an almost joke-free zone, although there was much giggling when Miranda popped her head into view through the window, upside down. They passed the last couple of hours singing show tunes, which they rather enjoyed, although none of them were in tune and 'howling' might be a better description. It certainly didn't do Mr McNumpty's headache much good.

Eventually they arrived at their destination, the Sunnyside Campsite at St Ives in Cornwall. It was a very pleasant spot, with plenty of room for lots of happy campers and a small shop selling fresh milk and the sorts of things people forget to pack – like toothbrushes, loo rolls, sun protection cream and tinned soup. There was a crèche for when parents and children needed a break from each other; toilets and showers; a playground; and a club room for dancing, sing-a-longs, bingo and other entertainment in the evenings.

The Bolds chose an area under a clump of pine trees, with the sandy beach and the sea just a short walk away along a grassy track – and decided to pitch their tent there.

One of the benefits of spending the holiday masquerading as a dog was that Bobby didn't have to help with any of the unloading or tent erecting. As soon as they got there he was off, bounding around the other tents, chasing about with the other dogs, sniffing and having a lovely time.

Betty was furious. She was having to unpack the car and collect wood for the camp fire.

'It's so unfair,' she shrieked. But as her mother reminded her: 'Trumpy is a dog. And doggies do what doggies do.'

'And he's doing a doggy-do-do right now,' pointed out Mr McNumpty. 'Go on, Betty, dear. You'd better go and clear it up.'

So as Betty and Minnie trudged back and forth, and Betty had to pick up Trumpy's 'business' in a poo bag, Bobby had a whale of a time. A little wire-haired Jack Russell called Taxi chased him round the campsite and down the grassy track and there, suddenly, was . . .

... the sea!

Bobby had never seen the sea before and he stopped and gasped. 'Wow!' he couldn't help but exclaim at the vast sapphire-blue expanse glistening in front of him, like a watery field of jewels.

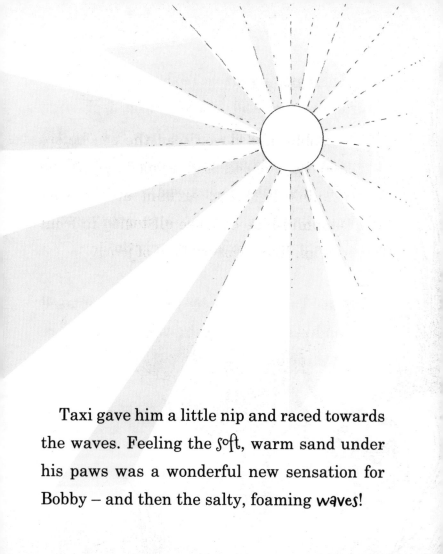

Taxi gave him a little nip and raced towards
the waves. Feeling the soft, warm sand under
his paws was a wonderful new sensation for
Bobby – and then the salty, foaming waves!

He plunged in after Taxi, the cool water easing his leg and making him feel wide awake after the long journey in a hot car. He had enjoyed swimming in ponds before – but never in a beautiful, endless sea! The only thing missing was Betty, but of course Bobby would never admit that. Brothers rarely do.

But as Taxi and Bobby played and chased and tumbled around in the water, they were being watched.

Watched by creatures you and I have probably never met. Creatures we would probably like to meet. And creatures we will eventually meet in this story . . .

So just be patient.

Chapter

Meanwhile back at the Sunnyside Campsite the rest of the Bolds were standing around the unpacked tent scratching their heads. The tent – metres of blue and orange canvas – was billowing about in the sea breeze while Mr Bold and the others held up various hollow steel poles amongst the pine needles and wondered how on earth they were supposed to fit them together. Several nearby campers watched with amusement. A few of them had felt similarly confused about their own tents when *they* had arrived.

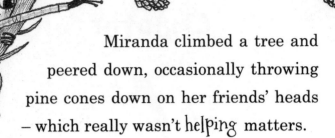

Miranda climbed a tree and peered down, occasionally throwing pine cones down on her friends' heads – which really wasn't helping matters.

'Aren't there any instructions?' asked Minnie.

'It's a second-hand tent I got at a boot fair,' explained Mr Bold. 'The man said we wouldn't need any instructions! It was all perfectly straight forward.'

'A-ha!' cried Mr McNumpty, who had successfully slotted one pole into another.

'But if we don't know what sort of tent it is and what it's supposed to look like, how do we know where to start?' was Minnie's next question. 'I mean, is it a tepee? An A-frame? An igloo?'

There was an awkward silence.

'This is intense,' said Betty.

'Ha ha!' laughed Mr Bold. 'See what you did there? Intense – in tents?' Everyone laughed politely, but joking wasn't, for once, going to help the situation.

Uncle Tony picked up some of the canvas, found a window in it and poked his head through. 'Yoo-hoo!' he said weakly.

Mr McNumpty and Minnie were the most sensible in the party, so they paired up to try and make sense of things.

'You fitted two poles together, didn't you?' Minnie reminded Mr McNumpty.

'I did, yes,' said Nigel proudly.

'Well, let's carry on with the poles and then maybe it will take shape.'

'Good plan,' he agreed. 'All poles over here, please!'

Betty and Mr McNumpty busied themselves collecting the aluminium poles that had been scattered about, then laid them in a row as directed by Minnie. She and Mr McNumpty began to tentatively try and slot them together.

'I'll unpack the camping stove and see if I can make us all a nice cup of tea,' said Mrs Bold.

'I'll have a rest,' decided Uncle Tony, and he sat against the tree trunk and closed his eyes.

Just then a soaking wet Bobby galloped back to them, panting with excitement, and then shook himself, spraying salty water over everyone.

'Oh, Bob— I mean, Trumpy!' complained Betty. 'You naughty boy!'

Mrs Bold checked Bobby's injured leg and put a clean, dry bandage on it, then poured Bobby a nice big bowl of water, which he enjoyed lapping up noisily, before sitting himself next to Uncle Tony in the shade for a nice rest.

'Aren't you going to help?' asked Betty crossly, but Bobby just shrugged at her.

'Dogs can't help put up tents, silly,' said Mr Bold, aware that their neighbours might be listening. 'Whoever heard of such a thing? Animals aren't that clever, remember.'

'Let's have a break for tea and doughnuts,' suggested Mrs Bold, holding the teapot. 'Or there's lemonade if you prefer.'

Bobby's ears pricked up at the sound of lemonade and doughnuts. He stood up expectantly. Betty shook a finger at him. 'Dogs don't drink lemonade, remember!' she told him with glee. 'Have some more water and a dog biscuit if you're hungry.' Bobby lay back down, his stomach rumbling. There were some disadvantages to being a dog, after all, he decided.

After tea, lemonade and doughnuts, Minnie and Mr McNumpty persevered with their attempts at putting up the tent. They had joined most of the poles together now, it was true, but it didn't look very tent-like. More like a wonky fence, or a piece of wobbly, rather dubious, modern art.

'Well, I think that looks very – er – interesting!' declared Mr Bold proudly. 'Much nicer than a boring tent!'

Minnie sighed. 'Oh dear. It's almost impossible!'

'Always nice to be different,' said Uncle Tony, waking up from his nap. 'No one else has a tent like that, do they?'

'True,' said Minnie, without conviction. 'Maybe it will look better once we put the canvas bit over the poles . . .'

'Let me take over,' said Mr Bold. 'You two have done enough.'

The construction was rather tall, so after several failed attempts at throwing the canvas high enough, with lots of huffing and puffing, Fred got on top of the car and threw the material over the poles. Everyone helped pull it down the sides then they stood back to look at their handiwork.

'Umm . . .' said Mrs Bold, lost for words.

The 'tent' was about two metres high, and seemed to veer off to one side rather dramatically for no particular reason, like a giant sock.

'Are you sure it's supposed to do that?' asked Betty.

'I think it's inside out and maybe upside down,' said Minnie.

'Well, it will be dark soon,' observed Mrs Bold. 'It'll have to do for now, I think.'

'Doesn't look like there's much room inside for us all to sleep,' commented Uncle Tony.

'That reminds me,' said Mr McNumpty. 'Where are the sleeping bags? I don't remember unpacking any from the car.'

Everyone looked expectantly at Mr Bold.

'Fred?' said Mrs Bold.

'Err . . .' said Mr Bold.
'Here's a joke . . .'

Did you hear about
the man who slept
with his head under
the pillow?

When he woke up he
discovered the fairies
had taken all his teeth!

'Very funny, dear. But where are the sleeping bags?'

'I brought my own,' said Minnie, rather primly.

'I didn't think we'd bother. Can't we all share Minnie's?' said Mr Bold.

'It won't fit eight, silly!' pointed out Betty.

There was a thoughtful silence.

'Suitcases!' exclaimed Mr Bold. 'That's it! Minnie can sleep in her sleeping bag and we'll all snuggle up together in the two big suitcases. It'll be' – he lowered his voice – 'like sleeping in the den back in Africa!'

So that is what happened. When they finally crawled inside the wobbly, strangely tall and

108

misshapen tent, Minnie – the only human in the camping party – slept soundly in her own sleeping bag and all the others piled into the suitcases with their clothes as blankets, some head to toe, some on top of others, but all of them laughing and giggling until they could keep their eyes open no more. All, that is, apart from Miranda, who was worried about getting squashed. She made her own special hammock out of a pair of Mr McNumpty's underpants attached over a metre above everyone else.

Before long all of them were sleeping soundly.

Chapter

And so, travelling done and tent put up (sort of), the next day the Bolds' much-awaited holiday began.

From the start, the people camping near to the Bolds thought them an amusing but rather odd family. (And they weren't wrong.) The Bolds seemed to find everything so funny – from their wonky tent to the way their funny-looking dog ate his dinner. Everything made them laugh.

But the field of cows next to the campsite knew, of course, that the Bolds were not really people at all. Animals recognise other animals when they see them, and those cows spotted a pack of laughing hyenas quite easily. There were fifteen cows in the field with their calves – a local breed called Cornish Red Rubies. On the first day they had all stood chewing grass in the field, listening to the Bolds' conversations and watching them try to erect their tent. One by one they lumbered over to the fence for a closer look, blinking and shaking their heads in disbelief.

'Good grief,' one muttered to another. 'Laughing hyenas trying to put a tent up. Whatever next!'

'And making a pig's ear of it,' replied the other.

'Ah, yes,' said the first cow. 'These must be

the famous Bolds. You must have heard of them. They sometimes take in unhappy animals and show them how to live as humans. They looked after a cow from Dorset called Kirsty once. Allergic to grass, she was, and they taught her how to be a secretary. I hear she now has a very good job at the BBC.'

'You don't fancy jumping over the fence and joining them, then?' asked her friend.

'Most definitely not. There's no better life than grazing in this lovely field, in my opinion. I'm very happy as a cow, thank you very much.'

And that, fortunately, was true of most of the animals in Cornwall. It is a very contented place. But this didn't mean the local animals weren't curious about these unusual holidaymakers in their midst.

Apart from the cows, sheep would look up when the Bolds passed by, seagulls swooped down to call out a greeting, foxes would hide behind trees to spy on them, and even mice would appear for a swift glance before darting away, laughing in their high-pitched, barely audible way.

Most friendly of all was a rather breathless puffin called Pamela, who met the Bolds on their first day at the beach. But more about her in a minute.

The beach and the sea was what the family had come for, and after an early breakfast outside their tent they gathered their beach bags and a picnic together and wandered off for a day at the seaside. As the sea came into view they all stood and stared in wonderment, just as Bobby had the day before.

'Wowser!' said Betty.

It was a glorious, warm sunny day on Sunnyside beach and there were lots of happy families swimming, sunbathing and generally enjoying themselves. The Bolds set up their windbreak, and a deckchair for Uncle Tony, then spread out their beach towels. Mrs Bold wandered down to the water's edge, holding up her skirt while she had a nice paddle. Trumpy chased Taxi around the sand dunes, and Betty and Minnie raced over to the rock pools and began collecting shells to make necklaces with. Mr Bold and Mr McNumpty decided to go off to find the crazy golf; Miranda went in search of an ice cream; and Uncle Tony settled himself into his deckchair to eat a sandwich and have a snooze.

Suddenly he was awoken by a flutter of wings as a puffin landed on his chair, tempted by the crumbs of his sandwich. She was a very neat bird, with black and white feathers and a bright orange beak and matching webbed feet.

'Pleased to meet you!' she said, speaking rather breathlessly, with a thick Cornish accent. 'I be Pamela and you're that family of animals from London-way, aren't you? Someone said you were in town.'

Tony introduced himself, then called to the others who were now all back and sunbathing on their beach towels – all except Miranda, who still hadn't returned with her ice cream.

Mrs Bold peeked over her very large sunglasses and invited Pamela to join them.

'That's very kind of you. Do you have anything else to eat?' Pamela asked, wheezing a little. 'I'm rather peckish.'

'I thought puffins ate fish?' said Betty.

Pamela nodded. 'You're quite right,' she replied. 'But I don't have the puff in me these days for long fishing flights.'

'Are you very old then?' asked Betty, getting straight to the point.

'Not really.' Pamela shook her head. 'But I'm known as Pam the puffing puffin. Would you like to know why?'

The Bolds all agreed that they would like

118

to know, and I suspect you would like to know too.

'I used to smoke cigarettes when I was a young puffling,' Pamela admitted. 'Very foolish thing to do, but I got in with the wrong crowd and I suppose I thought it made me look cool. Anyway, I regret it now, because it didn't do my lungs much good. Smoking is really bad for your health.' She's right, of course, and that's why children don't do it. You've got more sense. It's just some grownups who aren't clever enough to stop – some grownups and some puffins, it seems. 'So I get rather breathless these days,' continued the puffin. 'That's why the others call me Pam the puffing puffin. I don't have the puff in me to go fishing, let alone migrate to Iceland in the summer like most puffins.'

'Poor Pam!' said Mrs Bold. 'Have some of

our lunch, please. There are some crisps left, and how about a French Fancy?'

'Ooh, thank you,' said Pam, licking her beak. 'I don't mind if I do.'

'You're very welcome,' said Mrs Bold.

'And in return, I can be your holiday guide, if you like. Show you all the best places to visit. Beaches. Walks. Nice cafes for lunch.'

Everyone agreed that sounded like a terrific plan. Along with the sleeping bags, the Bolds had also forgotten to pack a guidebook for the holiday.

Chapter

Eventually Pam flew off and Miranda came back slurping at an ice cream that was almost as big as her. Goodness knows where she'd been. Uncle Tony was sitting in his deckchair again, gazing out to sea at the surfers.

'De-lish!' Miranda announced, as a big drip dribbled down her chin. 'You want?' She jumped onto Uncle Tony's knee. Tony nodded and helped himself to a rather generous slurp before looking back out longingly to sea.

'You like go swim-swim?' Miranda asked him kindly.

Uncle Tony nodded. 'Years ago, back in Africa as a hyena, I was a very good swimmer,' he told the little monkey.

'We finish ice cream. We go swim?'

'Well, I'm worried it might be a bit chilly for me, to be honest,' he replied. 'My bones are rather old these days. But it would be nice . . .'

'We hire wet suit! Keep Tony warm!'

'Maybe,' wondered Tony. Between them they finished the ice cream and then, without a word to the others, Miranda led Uncle Tony towards the beach hut where wet suits, flippers, snorkels and other equipment could be hired.

'Let's build a sandcastle!' announced Mr Bold suddenly. He was keen for some excitement after his visit to the crazy golf with Mr McNumpty had been cut short – Mr McNumpty had insisted on using his golf club to scratch his back, and Mr Bold's joke ('Why did the golfer wear two pairs of pants? Because he had a hole in one!') had not amused the other players and had rather put them off their game. The friends had been politely asked to leave.

Now Mr Bold began slipping out of his shirt and trousers to reveal bright red swimming trunks. Two rather well-groomed ladies sunbathing next to him wearing lots of jewellery and glittery bikinis, gave a muffled little scream when they saw how unusually hairy Mr Bold was. 'That reminds me,' said one to the other. 'I must collect my winter coat from the dry cleaners.'

'We'll build A HUGE sandcastle!' declared Mr McNumpty, rubbing his chin excitedly. 'A HUMONGOUS castle!'

'A sand palace!' said Mr Bold.

Mr McNumpty set to work, using his big paws to build a high mound of sand. There is no need for buckets and spades when you have big grizzly bear paws. He then flattened the top while Mr Bold tidied up the sides, patting them firmly. Soon Mrs Bold, Minnie and Betty had decided to join in the building project too.

Then Bobby, panting after another chase round the beach, came back and flopped down on a towel to rest and watch what was happening. He was rather close to the sunbathing posh ladies, who wrinkled their noses and muttered something to each other. Bobby thought he caught the words 'stinky' and 'mongrel'. The nerve! He loved pretending he was a dog, running about on all fours, his tail free to wag whenever it wanted to, but it was frustrating sometimes. Frustrating pretending he couldn't understand or indeed speak like humans did. He contemplated baring his teeth at the posh ladies, or even cocking his leg on their parasol, but he resisted. He had a strong dog-like urge to jump on top of the sandcastle, though . . .

'I know what you're thinking, Trumpy,' warned Betty. 'And you mustn't. Bad dog!'

Bobby rested his head on his paws. Betty enjoyed telling him off whenever she could, he realised. But he hadn't actually done anything **wrong** yet! He was coming to the conclusion that dogs get told off an awful lot. He dearly wanted to answer his sister back, but that wouldn't be possible with so many people about, of course.

After a while the castle was looking rather impressive. It had Gothic towers and turrets and lots of little windows decorated with shells and pebbles. They all stood back to admire their craftsmanship.

'Excellent work, everyone!' said Mrs Bold.

'I think something is missing, but I'm not sure what,' pondered Minnie.

'Doors?' suggested Betty.

'A drawbridge! That's it!' shouted an inspired Betty. 'Or rather, a MOAT!' Everyone agreed this was exactly what was required.

'Let's all dig the moat together, then it will be done in no time,' said Mr McNumpty, who was feeling a little tired.

'Trumpy can join in too,' said Minnie kindly.

Bobby leaped to his feet and wagged his tail enthusiastically.

So together they all began digging around the outside of the castle, and this time they used the buckets and spades Mrs Bold had brought – apart from Bobby, who dug with his front paws like a dog. They excavated so much sand between them there was almost enough to build another castle. It was thirsty work in the summer sun, so they stopped for a drink of water.

'Buckets and spades are too slow,' announced Mr Bold. 'Let's use traditional methods, like Trumpy's doing. It will be done much quicker!'

Everyone agreed and jumped into the moat. They began to dig, their front paws (or hands, in Minnie's case) pushing down, then flicking the wet sand out behind them. For the four Bolds and Mr McNumpty, a feverish animal digging-instinct began to take over and their paws dug faster and faster, deeper and deeper. They were all so engrossed in their task that they didn't worry about where the sand was going. Nor did they hear the cries from the posh ladies next to them who were now completely covered in sand.

Minnie stopped first. 'Oh no! I'm so sorry!' she said. 'I'll stop them.

Everyone, stop digging, please. STOP!'

Eventually she made herself heard and five sandy heads popped up from the moat like big curious meerkats.

'What's the problem?' asked Mr Bold.

'Er, our neighbours,' whispered Minnie, gesturing towards the ladies who were standing up now, furiously trying to shake the sand out of their previously perfect hair, and using their towels to wipe the sand that was unfortunately sticking to recently applied sunscreen on their arms, legs and faces.

'Awkward,' said Mr McNumpty.

Realising what had happened, Mr Bold immediately leaped forward and began to help with the removal of the offending sand. But this didn't really help matters.

'Get off me, you filthy, hairy beast!' one unfortunate lady screamed.

'Help!' squealed the other.

But Mr Bold kept apologising and trying to brush the sand off the ladies.

'Aaagh! Get your filthy paws off us!'

'Now don't overreact, madam. I'll have you clean in no time,' he insisted.

People nearby stood up, concerned, and a crowd began to gather. Then two lifeguards ran towards the quickly developing scene, blowing their whistles.

'What's going on here?' they asked.

'This beast has covered us in sand,' cried one of the ladies. 'Just look at us!'

'Beast?' said Mrs Bold, jumping to her husband's defence.

'Yes. Beast. He's a hairy beast,' said the other lady.

Mrs Bold was furious. 'Well quite frankly I think you two look a lot better now you're covered in sand. At least we can't see your ugly faces any more.'

'Please, ladies,' said Mr Bold. 'It's just been a misunderstanding.' He turned to the lifeguards. 'We were just digging a moat for our sandcastle – and I meant no harm in trying to help the ladies get the sand off.'

It took several minutes before the women

calmed down, at which point they packed up their things and moved well away from the Bolds in a huff. The lifeguards returned to their post and the crowd dispersed.

'Oh dear,' said Mrs Bold. 'I think we've spoiled their day. But who did they think they were, calling you a beast?'

Suddenly there was a cry from Minnie. 'Oh no! Our sandcastle is ruined!' The once magnificent castle was now reduced to a mushy mound of sand with a few shells scattered over it.

'The lifeguards must have jumped on it when they rushed over, I suppose,' said Mr McNumpty reasonably.

'Never mind. We'll build another!' said Mr Bold.

'Maybe not today, dear,' said Mrs Bold. 'We don't want any more trouble, do we?'

But Betty was staring at Bobby. He seemed to be covered in even more sand than before. And panting suspiciously. 'Trumpy? Did you have anything to do with this?' she asked accusingly.

'Woof!' he barked as innocently as he could.

Betty's eyes narrowed. 'I bet you jumped on the sandcastle when no one was looking, didn't you? Bad dog!'

This time Bobby was glad he couldn't speak. If he could, he'd have said something like: 'Sometimes a dog's gotta do what a dog's gotta do. And then do a doggy-do-do.'

Chapter 10

The Bolds hadn't been settled back on their beach towels for long before they were disturbed by a commotion from further down the beach — a collective cry of wonderment from a group of people gathered by the edge of the sea.

'I wonder what's going on there?' asked Mrs Bold, curious. Everyone forgot about the sandcastle and the unfortunate incident with the two posh ladies, and stood up, craning their necks to see what was going on. All along the beach, people were doing the same.

'Woooooo!' went the crowd, followed by a spontaneous round of applause.

'Let's go and investigate,' said Mr Bold, so they all hurried along the sand towards the throng of holidaymakers, who were looking out to sea.

Trumpy ran ahead.

It turned out that everyone was transfixed by the antics of a surfer who was riding the waves with great expertise and breath-taking skill.

'Wow! Amazing! Wow-ee!' cried the crowd.

When they got closer, the Bolds slipped through to the front so they could get a better look. None of the Bolds were very tall, although Mr McNumpty was much wider and taller than most people. He very obligingly sat down on the sand once they had found the spot with the best view.

'This dude is amazing!' a teenager next to the Bold party exclaimed. The 'dude' was at this time paddling back out to sea to catch the next wave and the Bolds hadn't yet had a clear view of his acrobatics.

'And the little kid with him knows what he's doing too,' commented someone else.

The Bolds could just about see the surfer in his wet suit, lying flat on his board, moving slowly out to sea, up and down over the swell, waiting for the right wave to come along. Then he chose a larger than average one, turned his board around and paddled quickly to gain speed.

139

The wave swelled and grew until it was bigger than any other. When his board was going fast enough and caught the thrust of the wave, the surfer got up on his feet and spread his arms to balance himself. Only then did the Bolds see the 'little kid' with him, standing on the front of the board, a miniature version of the surfer, expertly riding the wave.

Can you guess who it was?

Bobby recognised them first. It wasn't, was it? It couldn't be, surely? But of course he couldn't speak. He gave an excited, high-pitched bark instead and pawed at Betty's leg.

'Not now, Trumpy. I'm busy watching the surfers.'

Bobby barked again, but this time he half barked and half spoke. 'Wrrruff – Tgggrony – wruufff – Mirrruffanda!'

At last Betty understood. 'Mum! Dad!' she cried. 'It's Uncle Tony and Miranda!'

'Where, dear?' asked Mrs Bold.

'Out there, on the surfboard – that surfing dude and the little one – it's Tony and Miranda!'

'G-g-g-goodness, she's right,' said Mr McNumpty, shading the sun from his eyes to get a clearer view.

Just then the huge wave that Tony and Miranda were riding the top of began to change shape. It broke into a frothy wave at one end while the sea water spun around causing a barrel shape to form. Tony's board disappeared under the waves for a moment, and the crowd gasped and held their breath. But a few seconds later he reappeared inside the wave. This time there was a gasp of amazement. People held their smartphones high in the air to capture the wondrous surfing display they were witnessing. And as if this wasn't exciting enough, Miranda then performed a backward somersault and landed skilfully on Tony's shoulders. The crowd whooped and applauded.

The pair rode the wave, gaining speed, twisting and turning inside the barrel,

never losing their balance.

'These dudes are fearless!' said the teenager.

Next, Tony turned the board and they spun round in a complete circle inside the wall of water.

The Bolds watched open-mouthed, laughing with amazement.

'Unbelievable!' said Mr Bold, shaking his head.

Tony and Miranda then surfed gracefully out of the giant tube of water and glided smoothly to the shore on a fizzing last wave. The appreciative throng applauded loudly and crowded into the water to meet them, patting Tony on the back and lifting Miranda up on their shoulders triumphantly.

The Bolds rushed forward too, but it took them a while to get to the front.

Uncle Tony was now a little overcome by all the attention, and was sitting on the beach to recover, with Miranda on his lap. The crowd could now see that the 'dude' was in fact quite a hairy elderly chap, and everyone was all the more amazed.

Finally people began to wander off and the Bolds were able to rescue Tony and Miranda and usher them back to the campsite and the safety of their tent, where Tony sat on a fold-up chair and explained what had just happened.

'Well, I don't really know, if I'm honest,' he said. 'I was always a good swimmer back in Africa but I haven't done it for years and I've certainly never tried surfing before. But it just came so easily to me.'

'Really?' said Mrs Bold. 'But what about your arthritis? And you only learned to stand on your hind legs a few months ago. How on earth were you able to balance like that?'

'I don't know,' said Tony. 'It just happened.'

'You're a natural,' Betty said. 'Wow, Tony, that was so cool.' And she gave him a hug.

Tony looked very proud, but also a little bewildered. It was certainly very strange how easily he'd been able to surf. But for now his exertions that afternoon had clearly worn him out and his eyelids were beginning to droop. 'I've still . . . got it,' he managed to whisper, just before his head fell forward. The next second he was asleep with a faint smile on his face.

Miranda climbed gently onto his lap and rested her head on his chest, just as he began a contented snore. 'Tony tired. Tony sleep. Me too,' she sighed.

'And you're a great surfer too, Miranda,' said Mrs Bold quietly, as she placed a blanket over them before signalling for everyone to creep out of the tent and leave Tony and Miranda in peace.

Chapter

It was only then, when everyone was sitting outside the tent and Mrs Bold was boiling water on the little stove to make some tea, that they realised Bobby wasn't with them.

'Where's Trumpy?' asked Betty.

'Oh, his leg's so much better now, he's playing with Taxi, I expect,' said Mr Bold, unconcerned.

What did the dog say when he sat on some sandpaper?

Ruff!

'No, he's not with Taxi,' observed Mr McNumpty, ignoring Mr Bold's joke. 'Taxi is sitting over there, chewing on a squeaky toy.'

'Bobby was on the beach with us, watching the surfing,' recalled Betty. 'I expect he's chasing around the sand dunes again. I'll call him . . . Trumpy!'

This suddenly gave Mr Bold an idea for another joke.

What do you call a dog with no legs?

It doesn't matter what you call him, he still won't come!

Bobby didn't respond to Betty's call, so Mr and Mrs Bold, Minnie and Mr McNumpty, decided to go with her and look for him, leaving Uncle Tony and Miranda asleep inside the tent.

Mr McNumpty looked all around the campsite, calling: 'Trumpy? Trumpy!' in his deep voice as he went, and getting a few funny looks.

Meanwhile, on the beach, Mr Bold and Betty searched the sand dunes and Minnie and Mrs Bold walked all along the beach looking, calling and asking anyone they met if they'd seen a rather scruffy dog with a bandaged leg. But no one had. Eventually they all met up again back at the tent. Uncle Tony and Miranda had finished their nap and Minnie told them the worrying news.

'Me climb tree, looky long way,' said Miranda. Which she did, but she couldn't spot him.

'Maybe he's fallen asleep somewhere, just like me?' was Uncle Tony's suggestion. 'He has been running around a lot today.'

'But he wouldn't sleep for this long,' said Mrs Bold. 'He'd be hungry by now. It's almost his dinner time.'

'Perhaps he found a sandwich on the beach. Or a pork pie? I don't think we should worry,' said Mr Bold.

'I do. I am worried, Fred. We've lost our little pup! Wherever can he be?' said Mrs Bold, her voice beginning to tremble.

Fred put his arm around her. 'Now don't get

upset, Amelia. He's going to come bounding up that path from the beach in a moment, covered in sand and reeking of seaweed. Mark my words.' Everyone looked hopefully towards the path for a few moments, willing Mr Bold's words to come true. But there was no sign of Trumpy.

Mr McNumpty then had an idea and marched off purposefully to ask the Sunnyside Campsite manager to make an appeal over the loudspeaker. Minutes later, after a few loud clicks and bangs and a moment of high-pitched feedback, the announcement was made.

Ahem. Good afternoon, campers. This is the camp manager speaking. Or should I say the manager of the camp?

Er, anyways. It's about a lost dog. Not been seen for a couple of hours since. He's described as brown and black and grey with lighter splodges. Round ears, lots of teeth and a big, wet nose and has his rear left leg bandaged. No one would want to steal a dog like that, so he must be lost.

Trumpy's the name. The dog, that is, not me. He's of a friendly, playful disposition. As am I, but that's irrelevant.

Have you seen Trumpy? Could you please check your tents and trailers to see if he's maybe wriggled in somewhere he shouldn't have? Look under your cars. Anywhere you can think of. His owners are very worried about him. Trumpy. Missing.

If you find Trumpy please bring him AT ONCE to the camp manager at the camp office. Well, I mean the manager of the camp at the, er, site office. Thanking you.

The Bolds sat patiently for half an hour, waiting to see if any of their fellow campers had found Trumpy, but there was no news. While they waited they all called his name continuously, until they were quite **hoarse**.

'What shall we do?' cried Mrs Bold, tears streaming down her face. 'Perhaps the tide came in and washed him away. His leg is still not fully recovered and he's not as strong a swimmer as he should be.'

'Bobby, Bobby, wherever can you be?' said Mr Bold to no one in particular. He was feeling just as distraught as Mrs Bold but he was trying not to show it. He closed his eyes and concentrated. Where was Bobby? He had to be somewhere. There must be an explanation . . .

'Maybe it's a mistake to say we've lost a dog?' said Minnie. 'I mean – he's not a dog, is he?'

'He's not really a little boy either,' said Betty, stroking her arm. 'He's a' – she looked around to make sure no one outside of their group might hear her – 'a hyena.'

155

'We can hardly tell anyone that interesting fact!' said Mr McNumpty. 'Hyenas don't have a good reputation and everyone would think he'd escaped from a zoo or something.'

'We'll have to go to the police station,' said Mrs Bold decisively. 'It'll be getting dark soon. My son is out there somewhere, and whatever it takes to find him must be done. We'll have to tell the truth.'

'But that will mean the end of everything,' warned Mr McNumpty. 'Once they discover we aren't really people, do you suppose we'll be allowed to stay living in our nice houses in Teddington? Of course not. They'll have us out of there quicker than you can say Masai Mara.'

'I'll be sent back to the safari park!' wailed Uncle Tony.

'We all will!' joined in Mr McNumpty.

'It doesn't matter,' said Mrs Bold. 'What matters is that we get little Bobby back. I don't care where we live. As long as we're together.' She stood up and blew her nose, then inhaled loudly to calm herself. 'Come along, Fred. Let's get in the car.'

'You're right,' said Mr McNumpty. 'All that matters is that we find that pup.'

Mr Bold took several steps towards the car before suddenly stopping in his tracks. 'That's it!' he shouted. 'You're right. And Betty was right. Why didn't I think of it before!'

'What, dear? What didn't you think of?' asked Mrs Bold.

'We're hyenas, as Betty said,' replied Fred,

lowering his voice. 'What are hyenas good at?'

'Digging?' said Minnie.

'Scavenging?' said Mr McNumpty.

'Rubbing bum on plant?' squeaked Miranda.

'Smelling things?' said Betty.

'Exactly!' said Mr Bold, punching the air. 'We've been acting like humans for so long we've forgotten what we're really good at. Back in the wild, if we lost a member of the family we would put our noses to the ground and track their scent!'

'My goodness, you're right!' said Mrs Bold, clasping onto Mr Bold with desperate hope. 'I remember once, after a zebra hunt that had gone on for days, I lost the other members of

the clan. I just sat patiently by the watering hole and they found me. Hyenas' sense of smell is remarkable!'

Betty concentrated for a moment. 'I can smell Bobby now!' she declared.

'Yes!' said Mr Bold excitedly. 'That's the scent from when we were all here earlier. Now we just have to follow it.'

'And we'll find him?' asked Betty.

'For sure!' said Mr Bold, feeling proud that his daughter still had her hyena instinct intact, despite being born far away from the wild.

Uncle Tony tried to catch the scent too, but got a bit of fluff up his nostrils and had a sneezing fit. 'Oh dear. The old nozzle isn't what it once was,' he said.

Meanwhile Betty was indeed following her instinct: her nose pressed to the ground, she was already halfway to the beach. 'This way! Quick!' she yelled urgently.

'Hold up! One moment!' called Mr McNumpty.

The sight of what appeared to be a young 'girl' sniffing the ground so determinedly was already attracting titters from some curious Sunnyside residents, Mr McNumpty observed, so he came up with a rather ingenious plan.

A few moments later the Bold party set off to find Bobby. Betty was their chief sniffer, but her animal behaviour was hidden from view by a four-sided shield of towels, held in place by Mr McNumpty, Mrs Bold, Uncle Tony and Minnie. Mr Bold and Miranda meanwhile walked ahead, nodding and smiling at passers-by to distract their gaze. 'Evening!' he said cheerily. 'Just trying to, er, dry our damp towels while having a nice family stroll. Fancy a joke?'

What do snakes have embroidered on their bath towels?

Hiss and hers!

Meanwhile, every now and then, you could hear the muffled voice of Betty giving directions.

'Left! Left a bit more! Straight on!' And because Bobby had evidently been chasing about having jolly doggy fun, his scent was quite often leading them round in circles and figures of eight.

'Right!' came Betty's voice from behind the towels. 'Right again. In fact, keep going right. Now right again!'

The towel-holding party shuffled around, following instructions as best they could. Uncle Tony started to get dizzy at one point.

But eventually, after zig-zagging all over the beach and over and around the sand dunes, the scent led them in a straight line, right along the beach, past where the crowds had gathered to watch Tony and Miranda surfing, and along to the rock pools. Here the scent *suddenly* seemed to stop.

Their arms aching, the towel holders lowered Betty's shield, and everyone had a look around for Bobby.

They all sniffed the air, but the trail definitely seemed to have ended.

'Maybe he was so clean from swimming in the sea there was no scent left,' concluded Minnie.

Everyone tried calling again. 'Bobby! Trumpy! Here boy!' But to no avail. The sun was about to set on the horizon and there was neither sight nor smell of Bobby anywhere.

Mrs Bold sat despondently on a ledge. 'Oh, where can he be? Perhaps he fell into the sea? Perhaps he's drowned!'

'No no, not at all,' said Mr McNumpty. 'You mustn't think like that. You really mustn't. We know he's here somewhere,' he added, rubbing his chin thoughtfully. 'We must be patient.'

'He's probably waiting for us back at the tent,' said Betty, who was starting to miss her brother, even if he did make her cross sometimes.

'Betty's right,' said her father. 'Let's all go back to the tent. Perhaps Bobby's waiting for us back there.'

Chapter

The group trudged back to the campsite, but unfortunately there was still no sign of Bobby. Another announcement by the camp manager didn't get any results either. It was decided that going to the police and revealing their true identities was too risky – just yet. Mrs Bold agreed that they should rely on their animal instincts and animal friends to help find Bobby for now. Their whole lives and future depended on keeping their hyena identities hidden, after all.

'He'll turn up, the little rascal,' said Mr Bold.

Soon it was dark, and one by one the lights in all the tents were turned off as the campers went to sleep.

But it was a disturbed night at the Sunnyside Campsite. A pitiful howling began to echo around the pine trees, piercing the moonlit night.

'Hooooo-oowl! A-hoooowl! HOOOOW-OOOL!'

Hyenas have very strong family bonds and cannot bear to be separated. If one of their clan is missing it is the hyena way to call to them and so, in the middle of the night, Mrs Bold couldn't help but sit up in bed and howl for her lost son.

'Shurrup!'

'Keep the noise down!' shouted their neighbours crossly, but Mrs Bold's instinct would not be stopped.

'HooooWl! HoooooooWl!' she called.

In the end the camp manager came to see them, wearing his dressing gown and slippers, and told Mr Bold that there had been a lot of complaints about the noise.

'This awful racket has to stop, Mr Bold. It's giving some of my camp residents nightmares.'

'Mrs Bold is not feeling herself, I'm afraid,' said Fred.

'But she's howling like a wild animal!'

'I do apologise. Er, she's having a bad dream, you see.'

'Really?'

'Yes, keeps dreaming she's a dog.'

'How long has she been having these dreams?'

'Ever since she was a puppy.'

The camp manager gave Mr Bold a stern warning. 'Any more trouble and I'm afraid I'll have to ask you Bolds to leave.'

Mr Bold knew he couldn't allow that to happen. Bobby might never find them if they had to move to another campsite.

Minnie had heard all this and knew the best way to cheer up Mrs Bold and stop her howling was to come up with a plan of how they might find Bobby. After all, howling – unless Bobby was within earshot (and he clearly wasn't) – was not going to get any results.

'We need a proper plan, Mrs Bold. In the

morning, Miranda and Tony should search the beach again. I suggest that you, Betty and I make some "Missing Dog" posters with a picture of Trumpy on and put them up all around St Ives. Mr Bold and Mr McNumpty should go to the Dogs' Home. Bobby might have been mistaken for a stray and sent there.'

'A wonderful idea!' agreed Mr Bold.

'But we don't have any photos of Trumpy,' Betty pointed out.

'Then I could draw a picture. I'm rather good at drawing,' said Minnie.

'Oh, I do hope we find him!' wept Mrs Bold. But she did feel a bit better – or at least a little less like howling – now she knew there was something she could do. In fact, she couldn't wait to get started.

The next morning no one felt much like eating any breakfast, but Mr Bold said they would need to keep their strength up, so everyone had a bowl of cereal and some hot tea before the various parties went their separate ways, agreeing to meet back at the tent at tea time.

Uncle Tony and Miranda wandered along the beach, looking, calling and occasionally having a surreptitious sniff of the sand when no one was looking. Unfortunately lots of people remembered their surfing feats from the day before and their progress was constantly interrupted.

'Hey, dudes! Gonna spin some more waves?'

'You're so cool. Can we take a selfie with you?'

'Can you teach me some of your amazing moves?'

But eventually they made it to the far end of the beach where the rocks were. Sadly there was no sign of Trumpy anywhere. And the tide had been in since the night before, so even his scent had now disappeared. Tony gave a sigh and sat down to rest.

'Poor Tony. He no happy today,' squeaked Miranda, sitting down next to him. 'Me sad too.'

Just then there was a whirring, wheezing sound above them and in a shower of feathers, Pam the puffing puffin landed on the rocks beside them.

'Dydh da!' she said in Cornish. 'Good morning, folks!' She then had to stop to get her breath back.

'No. It's not a good morning, I'm afraid,'

said Uncle Tony. 'Trumpy has gone missing and everyone is frantic with worry.'

Pam looked concerned. 'Oh no,' she puffed. 'That is awful news.'

'Mrs Bold. She howl all night long,' Miranda informed the puffin.

'We've all split up into groups to search different places and ask if anyone has seen him,' Tony explained. 'But so far – nothing!' He lowered his eyes and gazed at a rock pool, as if hoping he might find the answer there.

Pam hopped onto Tony's knee. 'Listen,' she said. 'I have an idea. I can't fly very far because my lungs are no good. But let me go and speak to my puffin friends. Ask around. And the sea gulls! We'll do an aerial search – between us, we can cover all of Cornwall in no time!'

Tony looked at Pam, hope showing in his old eyes at last. 'Why, thank you, Pam. That will be a brilliant help!'

'Findy Trumpy! Findy Trumpy!' said Miranda, jumping up and down with excitement.

'We'll do all we can, I promise,' said Pam. 'Now I'll just take a few deep breaths before I fly off.' She opened her beak wide and inhaled as deeply as her damaged lungs would allow, spread her wings, and then up in the air she flew. 'Don't worry. I'll report back as soon as there is any news. Goodbye!'

And off she fluttered.

Chapter

Meanwhile Mr Bold and Mr McNumpty had arrived at the gates of the St Ives Dogs' Home. It was a large brick building on the outskirts of town. The pair followed the signs to the reception area and went inside to ask if any lost dogs had been handed in overnight.

You remember how I told you that the Bolds were people that unusual things happened to? Well, this was going to be one of those days. If *I* lost my dog and went to the Dogs' Home, they would either say, 'Yes, here he is!' or, 'Sorry, no we don't have any dogs of that description,' and that would be that. But for

Mr Bold and Mr McNumpty – nothing was that simple. Perhaps it's best if I just tell you what happened. Stand by.

The receptionist on duty that day was called Morenwyn, and she was just finishing off a muesli bar for her breakfast when Fred Bold and Nigel McNumpty walked in.

'Good morning,' said Morenwyn, wiping her hands on a tissue. 'You're here bright and early. How can I help you two gentlemen?'

'Ah, good morning, miss,' said Mr McNumpty with a smile. 'We've lost our dear dog, Trumpy, and wondered if he might have been brought here?'

'Do you have a photo of him?' asked the receptionist, turning to her computer screen and tapping noisily on the keys.

'Er, no we don't, I'm afraid,' shrugged Mr McNumpty. 'He hasn't been a dog for long. I mean, we haven't *had* him for long.'

Morenwyn glanced at Mr McNumpty. 'I see,' she said with a sigh. 'What does he look like?'

'I can answer that,' Mr Bold jumped in. 'He looks rather like me! Only smaller and, ahem, more dog-like.'

'Yes, they often say dogs look like their owners, don't they?' said a flustered Mr McNumpty.

'But you've only recently got him, you said?' frowned Morenwyn.

'Y-yes,' stuttered Mr Bold. 'But that's why I chose him. The spitting image of me as a pup, I mean boy. Uncanny . . .'

'Was he microchipped?'

'Ah . . . no. Well, yes. But it fell out.'

'A microchip can't fall out!' scoffed Morenwyn.

'Found it in his pyjamas one morning,' said Mr McNumpty vaguely.

'A dog in pyjamas?!'

'He feels the cold terribly,' improvised Mr McNumpty.

Morenwyn looked incredulous, took off her glasses and peered at the two friends.

'Now look,' she began. 'If you've just come here to be funny—'

Why did the elephant wear pink pyjamas?

Because his blue ones were in the wash!

'Oh no, here we go,' muttered Mr McNumpty.

Morenwyn wasn't impressed. She put her glasses back on and consulted her computer screen.

'So. You've lost a dog. He wasn't microchipped and you have no photo. All I can suggest is that you have a look around the kennels and see if you can find him. Through that door over there.' She sniffed and gestured to some swing doors at the far end of the reception.

'Thank you. Most kind,' said Mr McNumpty. He looked sharply at Fred. 'This way.'

Now the Dogs' Home at St Ives is perfectly fine. But dogs who are homeless or lost are not at their happiest. We all (dogs included) like a nice home to live in and kind people to look after us. That is what every resident of every dogs' home dreams about, after all. Now, you know that Mr Bold is a hyena and Mr McNumpty is a grizzly bear? And you know that animals everywhere recognise each other as animals and are pleased to see each other? And of course you know that the Bolds are famous in the animal world . . . So, for an actual member of the Bold family to turn up at their place of residence was like a pop star turning up at your school assembly. The dogs sensed their presence even before the swing doors opened to reveal the two celebrity visitors.

With their superior animal hearing, Mr McNumpty and Mr Bold heard the excited low-pitched whining. But nothing prepared them for the greeting they got once they entered the kennel area. I can only describe it as a euphoric happy, yappy hero's welcome. The dogs leaped up at the wire cages, tails whirring with delight, not barking so much as shouting – chanting even – 'Bold! Bold! Bold!'

In animal language they shouted their thanks to Mr Bold for all he'd done, rescuing animals and giving them new lives. They called him their champion, their idol, their saviour!

This unprecedented noise didn't go unnoticed, of course. The kennel workers, including Morenwyn, came rushing at once, wondering what on earth was going on.

Mr Bold and Mr McNumpty knew they didn't have much time. They thanked the dogs

for their kindness and adoration, but begged them to stay calm.

'Is my son Bobby here?' asked Mr Bold. 'Please tell me if you've seen him?'

But Bobby wasn't among the excited inmates of the St Ives Dogs' Home so Mr Bold and Mr McNumpty left quickly, before they caused even more of a rumpus.

Chapter

Uncle Tony and Miranda, Mr Bold and Mr McNumpty weren't having any luck in finding Trumpy, so that just left Mrs Bold, Betty and Minnie – whose job, you remember, was to put up 'Missing Dog' posters on lampposts and trees and in any shops that would be willing to display them.

As they didn't have any photos of Bobby as Trumpy, Minnie had drawn a picture of him and then written some information about him too.

'It's marvellous!' declared Mrs Bold, her lip

quivering at the resemblance of her missing boy. 'Just like him!'

The poster read:

LOST DOG:
HAVE YOU SEEN TRUMPY?

HE IS A VERY FRIENDLY, BROWN, WHITE AND BLACK
SPLODGY-COLOURED DOG WITH UNUSUALLY ROUND EARS,
BLACK EYES AND RATHER POINTY TEETH.

MISSING SINCE SUNDAY AFTERNOON.

HE IS MUCH LOVED!
IF FOUND, PLEASE CONTACT MR AND MRS BOLD
AT SUNNYSIDE CAMPSITE.

REWARD:
A LOVELY HAT HANDMADE BY MRS BOLD
AND FREE SURFING LESSONS FROM TONY THE DUDE.

'If anyone finds him I'll make the best hat ever!' declared Mrs Bold.

Next they went to the printing shop in St Ives High Street and had a hundred leaflets and posters made.

'Right,' said Mrs Bold. 'Let's get organised. Betty and Minnie, you stand outside the shops and hand out leaflets to passers-by while I go inside and charm the shopkeepers.'

'What do we say?' asked Betty.

'You say, "Excuse me, have you seen our little dog?" and give them a leaflet. Then ask if they could show their friends or maybe put the poster up in the street where they live.'

'Right-o!' said Betty.

'Be polite, remember!' Mrs Bold added, then disappeared into the first shop – a chemist's.

The man in the white coat behind the counter listened to Mrs Bold's tale of the lost dog and agreed that the poster could be put in his window.

'Yes, of course,' he said. 'I hope you find young Trumpy very soon. Er, while you're here, though . . . I can't help notice you have a rather hairy face. I've got some hair removal cream that could get rid of that for you, if you like? Just a thought.'

Mrs Bold stroked her face. 'Oh, **very** kind of you. But I

like my hairy face. Keeps me warm in the winter. Goodbye. And thank you,' and she hurried out of the shop. 'The nerve!' she laughed to Minnie and Betty when she joined them on the street and told them about the chemist's offer. 'Let's move along.'

The next shop was a greengrocer's, and they agreed at once to display a Trumpy poster – in fact, almost all the shop owners were only

too happy to oblige, and the shoppers of St Ives who Minnie and Betty gave leaflets to were very concerned too, taking posters home with promises to put them up in their front windows.

'Almost done!' said Mrs Bold when they reached the top of the high street. 'It's disappointing that no one's seen him but if Trumpy is anywhere around here I think we're bound to find him. Well done, girls!'

The last shop Mrs Bold entered was called Tiddles Tea Shop, where tired shoppers were enjoying Cornish cream teas, served to them by a smiling lady with large green eyes.

'Ah, good afternoon!' she purred. 'Welcome to Tiddles. My name is Bertha.'

'Hello,' said Mrs Bold. 'I wonder if you—'

But the lady interrupted her. 'Yes, of course. I've been expecting you. Have a table here at the back where it is nice and quiet, then we can have a private chat.' Bertha winked knowingly.

'Oh!' exclaimed Mrs Bold, following the instructions and settling herself in a chair at a round table with a frilly white tablecloth over it. The table was already laid with a pot of steaming tea and freshly cut sandwiches, and a two-tiered display of cakes and fancies. 'Thank you,' she said.

Bertha glided round to the other side of the table and sat down too. 'Dear Amelia,' she said. 'We don't have much time, so I'll be quick. You're looking for your missing son?'

'Er, yes. No. Yes. Trumpy, our dog, but . . . how do you know?'

Bertha glanced around the room to make sure no one was listening. 'Look into my eyes, Amelia. Look deep, deep into my eyes. Tell me what you see?'

Amelia had guessed already. 'You're one of us!' she whispered excitedly. 'An animal living in disguise!'

Bertha's smile got even wider. 'Correct. Have a sandwich.'

Mrs Bold was rather hungry, so while Bertha poured the tea she gulped down several ham sandwiches.

'Milk in your tea? Or cream?'

'Just a little milk please, Bertha.' Amelia had guessed that Bertha was a cat of some sort.

'I'm a cougar, my precious. Caught illegally in South America, I was kept as a pet when I was a kitten by a very rich and ruthless gangster – let's call him Mr X – in, ironically, Mousehole in Cornwall. When I grew up I was used to, shall we say, frighten his enemies . . . I'm sure you know what I mean.'

Amelia nodded. 'Humans don't like it when cats spit and growl.'

Bertha rolled her big green eyes. 'No, they don't. Not too keen on having my teeth sunk into their necks either.'

'So you were a bit like a guard dog?' asked Amelia.

'You could say that. But I'd rather you didn't.' Bertha's eyes narrowed. 'Anyway, the police eventually caught up with Mr X and he

was what they call "banged up". Locked away in prison for an awfully long time. He decided to set me free which was rather a shock, I can tell you. After a few months out on Bodmin Moor, I decided to get myself a more comfortable life, here in delightful St Ives. You Bolds were my inspiration. Hyenas in Teddington! Then why not a cougar in St Ives? I've been running Tiddles Tea Shop for two years now. Bliss! Friendly customers and all the cream I can drink.'

'But how could you afford to—'

'Jewellery. Let's just say the emerald collar my owner dressed me in was not imitation . . . And of course I know where the rest of the stolen goods and cash are buried, should I ever need a top up. Mr X always took me with him for protection . . .'

'Gosh,' said Amelia, glancing out the window to make sure that Betty and Miranda were OK. 'But how did you know about our Bobby?'

'Pam the puffin is one of my regulars. At least, she hangs out the back by the bins and I give her stale buns to eat. She flew in this morning in quite a tizzy and told me what had happened.'

'So she told you about Bobby?'

'Yes. And I was hoping you'd come in here today, because I have some information that might help,' said Bertha.

Just then a rather bad-tempered customer from the next table called out, 'Excuse me! Could we have some service here, please?'

Bertha glared over at the lady. 'Just a

miaow-ment please, madam!' Something in Bertha's stare made the woman shrink back.

'So what do you know about Bobby?' asked Amelia, desperate for any news.

'Well, I'd better be quick. I don't know anything specifically about Bobby. But I do know that he isn't the only dog to go missing from St Ives these last few weeks.'

'Really?' gasped Amelia. 'So there are others too!'

'Seems so. I hear all the gossip in here. I've heard three or four customers saying that their dogs have disappeared without a trace. Dogs of all shapes and sizes. There one minute. Gone the next.'

'How strange! Who would want to steal pet dogs?'

'There's only one person I can think of around here.'

'Who?'

'A very nasty and eccentric woman who lives alone on a boat at sea. She was an old friend of Mr X's. Not nice. She's known to be rather keen on dogs. Used to breed pedigrees once, I heard, before she was jailed for animal cruelty.'

'No!' gasped Mrs Bold. 'You think *she* might have Bobby?'

'I heard she was released from jail recently, so it's possible. But it's only a hunch and I'm afraid that's all the information I have. But maybe it will help you in some way.'

'Yes, yes, thank you! I appreciate it. What's this woman's name?'

'She's known as Dog-Mad Debby.'

Chapter

So, do you think Bertha was right? Could Bobby have really been taken by a cruel, evil dog-napper? Well, I'm sorry to tell you but the answer is yes.

And at that very moment, Bobby was hungry and shivering down in the hold of a boat with several other unhappy, poor dogs. He'd just spent the loneliest, scariest night of his life and he was sure things were going to get a whole lot worse.

Suddenly the hatch above his head opened and Dog-Mad Debby shouted down for all the dogs to get up on deck. 'Now! Quick march, or you'll get a good kicking!'

She was a stout woman with beady eyes and a hairy chin. Over her big, grubby coat she was wearing a stained polythene mac, and her matted hair was covered with a frayed headscarf tied tightly under her chin. She paced up and down in front of her captives like a sergeant major inspecting the new recruits. Tucked under her arm was a whip.

Bobby watched the woman warily. When he'd been playing on the rocks yesterday she had smiled at him, stroked him and given him a very tasty biscuit before starting a game of 'fetch' with a tennis ball. He'd realised later that she had simply been luring him closer and closer to her boat, because before he knew what had happened, she'd thrown a blanket over him and bundled him on board.

There had been no more smiles or biscuits after that – he'd been quickly sailed out to sea and locked in the hold with an assortment of other dogs, all with similar tales to tell. He was frightened, hungry and very homesick.

The smallest of the dog-napped dogs aboard with him was a quivering hairless little dog called Walter who had been stolen from his owner's handbag while she sunbathed on the beach.

'I always wear a woollen coat, because I'm a Chinese crested dog, and I feel the cold terribly,' he'd told Bobby. 'She – Debby – ripped my coat off me to blow her nose on. Now I can't stop shivering,' he said.

The other dogs did their best to keep little Walter warm, but it was damp and draughty in the hold of the boat. And now all six of them were tied up in a line on the rolling deck, and poor Walter was feeling seasick as well as freezing.

'Now then, my lovelies,' said Debby. 'Let's have a look at you. You all seem a bit sad. Cheer up! No one is going to want to buy a miserable-looking hound, are they? Look happy please, and then you'll get a posh new home. Look fed-up and I'll be forced to throw you overboard. Understand? You scratch my back and I'll scratch yours.' She stopped suddenly in front of Walter. 'You!' she shouted accusingly. 'What on earth am I supposed to do with you? What was I thinking, stealing an ugly mutt like you? No one will want a half-dead bald dog, will they? I've seen more meat on a butcher's apron.'

Poor Walter whimpered with cold and fright.

'SHUT UUUP!' screeched Debby. 'I think in the morning I'll chop you up with some tomatoes and make you into a nice spaghetti Bolognaise.'

She moved along the line and stopped in front of Bobby. 'Hmmm. Show me your teeth?' she demanded. Bobby obliged. 'Very healthy, I suppose. I can see potential in you,' she said, appraising him. 'Once I've added a few Debby touches!'

Bobby dreaded to think what Debby was going to do to him. Whatever plans she had, he doubted they would be very pleasant.

She was the nastiest, unkindest, meanest human he'd ever come across and he'd met some pretty horrible people in previous adventures.

As Debby carried on along the line, shouting at the other dogs, laughing in their faces or teasing them with dog biscuits that she then cruelly snatched away, Bobby was suddenly aware of a fluttering and panting behind him.

'Psst! Psst!' he heard someone wheeze. Turning his head, he was surprised and relieved to see Pam the puffin sitting on the side of the boat.

'Pam! Pam!' he whispered, making sure he didn't get Debby's attention. 'You've got to help me. I've been dog-napped by a crazy woman! I've had nothing to eat all day and I'm so thirsty.'

Pam breathed deeply a couple of times before she could reply. 'That's what I'm here for, *me 'ansome*. Your family's going out of their minds with worry. And all the local animals are looking for you.'

'How did you find me?'

'Some seagulls told me they'd heard a lot of barking coming from this boat so I came to investigate. But it was further out than I thought. I nearly didn't make it. I need to get my breath back first.'

'I'm so glad to see you,' said Bobby. 'But how are you going to get me off this boat? We don't have much time.'

'What d'you mean?'

'Well, from what the others say, she's stolen

us all and then she's planning to give us all a makeover so she can sell us to the rich people of St Ives who want pedigree dogs. She painted black spots on a white bulldog type and sold him off as a Dalmatian yesterday, and apparently last week she gave a sheepdog cross a perm and sold it as a poodle! Goodness knows what's she's got planned for me. I need to get off this boat quick.'

Just then Debby came walking back down the line. 'What's all this noise?' she shouted. 'And what's that ugly bird doing here? Go on, Shoo-Shoo!' she shrieked, flapping her arms at Pam.

Pam fluttered up into the
air but Bobby could see
she really didn't have
much puff left. Could she
seriously make it back to
shore and get a message
to his parents?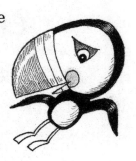

'Good luck!' he called after her. 'Fly safely!'

'I'll try, *me'ansome,*' she called back, battling
to fly against the blowing wind.

Chapter

Later that day the Bolds' search parties met back at the tent, each group hoping the other would have some news about missing Trumpy.

Uncle Tony and Miranda hadn't spotted him or found any new scent to follow.

Mr Bold and Mr McNumpty reported that Trumpy wasn't at the Dogs' Home either.

And no one had turned up at Sunnyside with any information as a result of Betty and Minnie's poster campaign.

The only glimmer of hope was the news Mrs Bold had received from Bertha the cougar about a strange woman called Dog-Mad Debby who lived on a boat somewhere.

'But where?' sighed Mr McNumpty. 'The sea is huge! It'll be like looking for a needle in a haystack.'

'Or a flea on a grizzly bear,' offered Mr Bold. 'No offence.'

Just then a familiar whizzing sound and a shower of feathers indicated that their puffin friend was dropping by. She lay on her back in front of the tent, beak wide open, gasping for air even more desperately than usual.

'Pam!' cried Uncle Tony. 'Whatever is the matter?' He gently helped Pam onto her feet. 'Take your time, little one,' he said soothingly,

gently stroking her back while her breathing gradually returned to normal.

'I-I-I flew as fast as I could,' Pamela explained, her eyes occasionally rolling to the back of her head. 'But it was almost too much for me.'

'You poor thing,' said Betty.

'Why? Is it something to do with Trumpy?' asked Mrs Bold anxiously.

Pam nodded. 'Saw him.' She gestured out to sea.

'On a boat?' prompted Mrs Bold.

Pam nodded once more.

'Dog-Mad Debby!' gasped Mrs Bold.

After a while Pam was able to explain. 'Some seagull chums tipped me off that they'd heard the sound of distant barking coming from a boat moored off Harlyn Bay. A small fishing boat with a red hull and a white painted deck, they said, anchored out at sea. So I flew around till I found it. It was further out than I'd thought. And they were right. I found several dogs on board, all looking very miserable and each tied with rope to the buoys and anchor on deck. One of them was Trumpy!'

'No!' cried Mrs Bold.

'Poor Trumpy! Was he hurt?' asked Betty.

'Not as far as I could tell,' said Pam. 'Bit bedraggled, though. Frightened, obviously, and chacking.'

'Chacking?' repeated Mr Bold.

'Thirsty,' explained Pam. 'Local word for thirsty.' She sucked in a breath. 'He asked me to come and find you, explain where he was.'

'Thank you, Pam. Thank you so much,' said Mrs Bold gratefully.

'But how did he get on the boat in the first place?' asked Minnie. 'And who were the other dogs? Who owns the boat?'

'I be getting to that, *me 'ansome*,' replied Pam patiently. 'Saw her with my own eyes, I did. A mazed, stuggy benyn!' she said dramatically.

Everyone looked confused.

'A mad, sturdy woman!' Pam clarified.

'Dog-Mad Debby!' announced Mrs Bold excitedly. 'Bertha was right! We must go to Harlyn Bay at once and rescue my poor boy.'

'And what's this dog-mad woman planning to do with Bobby?' asked Mr McNumpty.

'She's going to give him a cruel makeover to make him look like a posh dog and then sell him off to some rich, and quite frankly unobservant, people in St Ives.'

'What on earth could she turn Trumpy into?' pondered Betty. 'He's never going to look like a pedigree dog in a million years. A floor mop, perhaps!' She chuckled to herself, despite the seriousness of their situation.

But her mother gave her a look.

'There's no time to lose then,' said Mr Bold. 'Quick, everyone, to the car.' They all stood up, rushed to the Honda and squeezed in. Pam perched on the dashboard and directed them to the sleepy cove from where they could see the boat. As they travelled along, not even Mr Bold was in the mood for any jokes.

In the fading light, he parked the car and they all raced down the beach to the salty sea edge. There, outlined on the horizon, they could see Dog-Mad Debby's boat anchored some way out and just hear faintly the distressing sound of far-away dogs, barking for their owners.

The beach was deserted and unfortunately there weren't even any boats at anchor there. As the Bolds looked dismally out towards the

sea, the problem of how they were going to
reach Debby's boat began to dawn on them. A
big full moon rose in the sky, its silvery light
reflected on the still water.

What do you think the Bolds could do? It was too far out to swim – and there were no waves for Uncle Tony to surf on. Even if there were he couldn't rescue Bobby single-handedly – he was too old . . . Who was going to help?

As I told you before, though, unusual things happen to the Bolds – and something *very* unusual (and rather wonderful) was about to occur.

Chapter

The friends all stood in a line at the water's edge: Mr and Mrs Bold, Mr McNumpty – with Pam the puffing puffin on his head – Uncle Tony, with Miranda perched on his shoulder, Betty and Minnie. They were thinking as hard as they could.

'Well, I've had an idea,' said Mr McNumpty, not sounding very convincing. 'Debby can't stay out at sea for ever. We could wait here until she comes ashore to sell the dogs, then jump aboard and get Bobby.'

'But that might be days!' responded Mrs

Bold after an uncomfortable silence. 'Or she might sail further away. Or go to another cove. Or sail to Australia! My Bobby needs rescuing now. We must get to him as soon as possible.'

'What about the Coastguard?' suggested Betty.

'They do search and rescue and maritime emergencies,' said Minnie, shaking her head. 'They wouldn't be interested in a lost dog. Anyway, he's not lost, as we know where he is.'

'He's not a dog, either,' muttered Betty.

'Hire a boat?' said Uncle Tony.

'There aren't any. And we couldn't sail it anyway. Not after dark,' said Mr McNumpty.

The group lapsed into worried silence. Every

now and then a ghostly howl floated over the
sea from Debby's boat . . .

It was Minnie who saw it first. 'What is that?'
she said quietly, raising an arm to point at
something in the water just a few metres out
from the shore.

'Where? I can't see anything,' said Betty.

'There it is again!' exclaimed Minnie. A
small triangular shape broke through the
surface of the water, then disappeared again.

'Me see it!' said Miranda.

'Probably just a bit of driftwood,' said Mr
McNumpty dismissively.

'No, it's moving too fast,' disagreed Minnie.

'Hang on – there are a few of them now,' said Mrs Bold. 'Look!'

It was true. Six or seven of the shapes now rose out of the water in a line, shot along for a metre or so and then submerged again.

'Looks like they might be fish of some sort, perhaps?' pondered Mr Bold. Everyone had seen them now. The shapes changed course so they were moving in a circle right in front of them, causing graceful ripples to radiate outwards.

'It's as if they are trying to get our attention,' said Minnie. Everyone moved closer, up to their knees now in the sea. And then, to gasps from the Bolds, a big, blue-grey head appeared in the centre of the formation, with a wide smiling mouth and a row of neat pointed teeth. Large, black, wide-set eyes looked kindly at them.

'A *dolphin*!' whispered Betty. 'Oh my goodness!'

'Why hello, everyone!' said the dolphin, speaking in a clear, friendly way. 'It is quite exceptionally pleasant to make your acquaintance. My name is Galileo. And you, of course, are the Bolds.' He spoke in a very posh voice – more of a drawl, in fact.

'Er, y-y-you know who we all are?' stuttered Mr Bold.

'My dear Fred, your work rescuing animals from drudgery is world-famous! Of course I know who you are.'

The Bolds glowed with pride.

'Nice evening for a swim, isn't it?' said Fred.

'Oh, Mr Bold!' said the dolphin, chuckling. 'You are an amusing fellow. Your humour both entertains and enlivens all who hear it. And as for your Christmas cracker jokes – they are very popular here in the Cornish faction of the bottle-nosed dolphin community. Simultaneously predictable and innovative, preposterous and enlightening, foolish yet educational. Bravo!'

'Thank you!' said Mr Bold, a little confused by all the big words.

'I couldn't trouble you for a dolphin joke, could I?' continued Galileo. 'My friends and I would be unspeakably thrilled.' Five other eager dolphin heads appeared out the water, all looking expectantly at Mr Bold.

'Oh, I'm sure I could come up with something. Er, let me think now . . .'

Did the dolphin break the vase by accident?

No, he did it on porpoise!

The six dolphins laughed appreciatively – a nasal, high-pitched snort of a laugh, and applauded, daintily clapping their rubbery fins together to create a rather squelchy noise.

'Any more? We did so appreciate that. Encore!'

'Of course,' said Fred. 'Here's another one.'

What did
Cinderella dolphin
wear to the ball?

Glass flippers!

This went down even better, and as well as applaud, two of the younger dolphins leaped in the air and did a somersault to show how much they had enjoyed the joke, landing with a loud splash.

Mrs Bold had had enough. She marched into the water and tapped her husband on the shoulder. 'May I remind you, please, that our son is out there on that boat, crying and whimpering and wanting a hug from his

mum?' she said crossly. Next she turned to
the dolphins. 'It's lovely to meet you, and I'm
glad you enjoy my husband's jokes. But we
don't have time for this. Having fun will, for
once, have to wait. Some awful person called
Dog-Mad Debby has kidnapped, or dog-napped
or hyena-napped, or whatever-you-want-
to-call-it-napped our pup Bobby. Now will
somebody please . . .'

DO SOMETHING!

Mrs Bold bared her teeth at the dolphins. Her eyes seemed to glow an angry red as her maternal hyena instinct to rescue and protect her young showed itself with unmistakable ferocity. Several of the dolphins sank below the water.

'It's all right, dear. Keep calm. We'll think of something,' said Fred as soothingly as he could.

'WHAT?' growled Mrs Bold.

'My dear Amelia,' said Galileo. 'But that's why we are here. We have come to help!' he said. 'Forgive us, we got carried away with the excitement of meeting your husband and his entertaining *amuse-bouche*.'

'How are you going to help us?' asked Mr McNumpty, not unreasonably.

'We will transport you to the boat. On our backs. That's how,' replied Galileo. 'We have been watching your son Bobby, or Trumpy as he's sometimes called, swimming about with the playful young Taxi. Oh, and thumbs up (not that we have been blessed with those particular digits) to Uncle Tony and Miranda for their surfing – an amazing display!' There was more applause from the other dolphins, who had reappeared once Mrs Bold stopped shouting.

'We may have helped propel the surfboard a little from under the water, using our dolphinesque expertise and unseen by anyone, but really, all credit to you.'

'You mean you helpy-ed us with our surfing?' said Miranda.

Uncle Tony looked
a little crestfallen at
this news.

'Yes, my dear,'
confirmed Galileo.

'So I wasn't a
natural after all,'
said Uncle Tony
rather sadly.

'Well, I still think
you're brilliant,' said Betty.

'We just gave you a helping hand – or
should I say flipper? But you do have some
natural talent, I'm sure. You see, we've been
watching out for you since you arrived. It's
just a trifle unfortunate that we were having
our afternoon nap when Debby took a liking

to Bobby and nabbed him while he was sniffing about the rocks. He had a bit of a poorly leg, didn't he? Don't suppose she'd have caught him otherwise. Now then,' continued Galileo. 'To matters in hand: the liberation of your offspring. We'd be delighted to help. There are six of us and seven of you.' He looked kindly at Pam. 'Plus this lady, of course. You hop on our backs – Tony and Miranda can share a dolphin – and we will slowly and silently swim alongside Betty's boat. Once you all climb aboard, it's over to you to rescue young Bobby and get him away from Dog-Mad Debby. Do you think this will be of any assistance to you?'

'Brilliant! Thank you so much!' said a delighted Mrs Bold.

'I've always wanted to swim with dolphins,' said Minnie.

'We'd come on board with you, but frankly, a school of dolphins flapping about on the deck is not going to help matters. We'll wait in the sea till you've liberated Bobby and then bring you all safely back to the shore.'

Mr Bold was rubbing his chin thoughtfully. He loved this plan but as you'll know if you've ever read any other of the Bolds' stories, Mr Bold is an excellent plan-maker himself and he was about to add some finishing touches of his own to Galileo's idea.

'Is there a big rock sticking out of the water just past where Dog-Mad Debby's boat is moored?' he asked. 'I thought I saw one . . .'

'Yes, there is,' confirmed Galileo.

'Excellent. Then I think I have a plan!' said Mr Bold. 'Give us ten minutes while I brief everyone and get a few things from the car, and then we'll be ready.'

'Perhaps another joke to keep us amused while we're waiting?' asked the dolphin.

'Very well,' said Mr Bold, glancing warily at his wife.

Er . . . what do you call a fish without an eye?

Fsh!

Chapter

Do you want me to tell you the whole plan? I'm quite sure you do. But I think if I do that it will take away the surprise and you'll find yourself putting this book down to watch something dreary on television. So I'm going to keep you in suspense a little longer, I'm afraid. But trust me. It's a great plan.

A short while later the rescue party set off. It was quite a sight: in accordance with Mr Bold's instructions, Betty went ahead on the first dolphin, and the others followed. But you wouldn't have recognised them – they had all had a roll in the mud to make themselves look darker and therefore less noticeable in the moonlight, and Mr Bold had covered everyone in long slimy strands of seaweed too. Once they were all astride their assigned dolphin, they clasped their ride with their thighs, a bit like horse riding, and leaned forward to keep hidden. It was quite a fishy sight, as the procession glided quietly towards its destination.

'Claws crossed we get there in time!' whispered Pam, hopping onto Mr McNumpty's shoulder after they had been in the water for only a few minutes. 'Don't mind if I hitch a lift, do you?' she puffed. 'I've done enough flying today to last me a week.'

'Be my guest,' said Mr McNumpty, giving Pam a gentle stroke on her back.

Meanwhile Betty's dolphin took her to the rock near the boat, as her father had planned. She clung on tightly to her dolphin taxi as they approached the boat. He told her to take a deep gulp of air as they were going to be travelling underwater for about thirty seconds. When they reached the surface again, they'd passed Debby's boat and were hidden on the far side of the rock.

'Here you are. Good luck!' whispered the dolphin, and Betty crawled onto the craggy outcrop. She lay low, motionless, waiting for the signal from Pam the puffin, as arranged.

Everyone else in the dolphin convoy, meanwhile, had silently arrived at the stern of the boat, in easy reach of the ladder. They sat still on their respective dolphins, tense with excitement.

Everything was in place, and Mr Bold's plan to rescue Bobby was about to s p r i n g into action.

He peered over his shoulder to see if everyone was ready, then he nodded gravely at Miranda who nimble-hopped onto his shoulder and from there to the ladder. Next he gave a hand signal to Pam the puffin, who fluttered up into the air and flew, just above the water, round the boat to the rock where Betty was waiting, poised and determined. Pam bounced up to the hyena pup and said, 'You go, girl!'

There was no going back now, thought Betty. It was now or never!

Chapter

Dog-Mad Debby had just finished what she was doing to Bobby and was standing back to admire her handiwork.

'Yes. Brilliant if I say so myself. You are now just the sort of dog some stupid, rich idiots will want to adorn their luxury homes with. You, my lovely, are going to earn me a small fortune. One of my best-ever forgeries! I just have to fake the Kennel Club paperwork and tomorrow I'll shove you in a crate and sell you to the highest bidder at St Ives market. Then with the money I'll buy myself a nice new handbag and a bottle of champagne.' She suddenly swung back round to poor Walter. 'Something to wash down my spaghetti Bolognaise with!' she shouted. 'Happy days!'

Bobby's hopes of being rescued were fading fast. Could poor Pam really have got a message to his family? And even if she had, how could they rescue him? And would they even recognise him now that he looked so different?

When the low mournful howl started, to begin with Debby thought it was coming from one of the dogs on the deck. 'Stop that!' she said. 'Who is making all that din?' Then she realised it was coming from somewhere nearby. She shuffled over to the rail and looked out to sea. 'Who's there?' she called.

'Whooooh!' came the pitiful howl again. 'Whoooh! A-whoooh!'

Debby thrust her gnarled hand into her coat pocket and pulled out a pair of binoculars. She scanned the horizon, but it was now too dark to see. So she put the binoculars away and listened again.

'AWOOOH! HOWWWOOO!'

The cry was louder now. Realising it was coming from the other side of the boat, Debby ran to the opposite deck and peered out across the still water. There, silhouetted against the moon, she saw it – a dog, maybe a puppy –

standing on top of the nearby rock, its head tilted towards the stars. Can you guess who it was? Yes that's right. Betty!

'Ah!' said Debby. 'How on earth did a dog get there?' She glanced back at the faraway shore. 'Any dog who can swim that far must be a very fine specimen indeed! And that voice! If I can catch it and sell it as a guard dog I'll have enough money for a crate of champagne!'

She rubbed her hands together. 'I'll row over and collect it on my dinghy,' she muttered to herself, before herding, pushing and kicking all the other dogs on the deck back down into the hold. Then she locked the door and, wheezing with excitement, turned the winch which lowered her small inflatable boat down to the water. Unsteadily she jumped in and untied the ropes.

All this time the wolf-like cries continued from the dog on the rock. 'Be patient, my lovely,' muttered Debby as she rowed towards the barren islet. 'Debby is coming for you. Won't be long now . . .'

Once Dog-Mad Debby was on her way, the second part of Mr Bold's plan sprang into action. Miranda held the ladder in place while first Mr and Mrs Bold, then Mr McNumpty, Uncle Tony and Minnie climbed on board. Miranda shimmied to the top of the mast to act as a lookout.

When they were all safely on the deck, Mr Bold held his finger to his lips. 'Shhh!' He indicated that they must make no noise whatsoever. But even at a time like this he couldn't resist telling a joke.

Then everyone had to try and laugh silently, which as you may know, is **very** difficult to do. In fact, knowing you can't laugh or make any noise usually makes you laugh all the more. This is what happened, until Mrs Bold almost keeled over, hugging her chest with one arm and covering her mouth with the other. Even so the occasional cackle escaped, but the fear of being discovered by Debby quickly sobered them up. A few seconds later everyone had recovered themselves enough for the serious business of the rescue to begin.

As they listened to the fading sound of the dinghy approaching the rock where Betty stood howling away, Mr Bold pulled himself together and reminded everyone that there was no time to lose.

'Bobby is on board this boat and we're not leaving without him,' he said.

Suddenly they were all aware that Betty's howling had stopped, which could only mean one thing. Debby had reached the rock – and Betty! Puffin Pam fluttered down to tell them as much.

'Debby . . . rock . . .' she managed to say. 'Quick!'

Mr Bold had instructed Betty to play for time. If Dog-Mad Debby had gone to all the trouble of rowing over to the rock he was sure she wouldn't leave without her new acquisition.

'We'd better get on,' said Mr McNumpty impatiently. 'Where has she put Bobby?'

Uncle Tony sniffed the air. 'Below deck,' he said.

Led by Mr Bold, they clambered down the ladder to the hold. Mr Bold pressed his face to the door.

'Bobby?'

'Dad?'

'Yes, son. We're here to get you out. Don't make any noise.'

'OK,' answered Bobby, his voice quivering with emotion. 'But the door is locked. And it's not just me in here. There are SIX of us!'

Chapter

20

Debby had landed on the rock and was creeping up towards Betty.

'Good dog, don't worry!' she said, her tone suddenly transformed into a kindly, motherly voice, reassuring and enticing. 'Come to Debby, good dog!' In her pocket was a large net. As soon as she got close enough she planned to throw the net over Betty – a technique she had used many times before. Once covered in the mesh, Betty would be helpless. Her captor would simply pull a rope, tighten the net, and drag her prize towards her like a spider snaring a fly.

Betty played for time, moving as far away from her pursuer as the rock would allow. She perched on the edge, as if contemplating a dive into the water and a swim back to the shore, which caused Debby to back off, wait and try to reassure the object of her desire.

'Good dog! Biscuit?' Debby reached into her pocket and pulled out some tasty doggy treats. She held them in the palm of her hand and reached out towards Betty. 'Here!' she cooed encouragingly.
'What's this then?'

Betty pretended to be interested, all the while keeping one eye on the boat moored a couple of hundred metres behind Debby. She could just about see some figures creeping around on the deck but she knew the rescue wasn't over yet. She needed to string things out with Debby for a bit longer.

Over on Dog-Mad Debby's boat, the dogs locked down in the hold began to bark excitedly when they heard a rescue attempt was underway, so Bobby calmed them all down and tried to keep them quiet.

'Stand well away from the door, please!' said Mr McNumpty. 'I'm going to have to batter it down.' He took a few paces back then charged, his shoulder forward, towards the cabin door. There was a loud thud, but the lock held firm. 'Oof!' said Mr McNumpty. 'I'll try again.'

On his third attempt there was a satisfying splintery crunch and the door flew open. The dogs were cowering at the far end, and Walter was covering his ears with his paws.

'Bingo!' said Mr McNumpty, rubbing his shoulder.

'Everyone all right in here?' asked Mr Bold, casting his eye over the motley collection of mutts.

'Bobby?' said Mrs Bold, worried still. 'Where's my Bobby? I can't see him.'

A long-haired blond creature shuffled forward. 'I'm here, Mum,' he said.

The voice sounded familiar, but this creature didn't look anything like Bobby. Uncle Tony shone his torch over the dog from head to toe. The dog's head was one big, ginger-ish pom-pom with two eyes popping through, and you could just about see his four feet underneath the long ash-blond ringlets that grew from his back right down to the ground. Behind him hung a very limp, string-like tail that was so long it trailed about thirty centimetres behind him.

Minnie spoke first: 'What on earth?'

'What has that evil woman done to my baby?' cried Mrs Bold.

'She has made me into an Afghan hound, that's what,' said Bobby crossly. 'Can someone please get this horrible wig off my head and remove this silly, hairy onesie? It's very itchy.'

By now Mr Bold had started giggling, and it was very infectious. 'He looks like a Persian cat that's been through a washing machine,' he said.

'He has rather let his hair down!' quipped Uncle Tony.

Everyone was starting to laugh now, including the other captured dogs. Shrieking, whooping laughter that got steadily louder and louder.

Just then Miranda leaped into the room. 'Quick,' she said. 'Debby on way back! She hear you laughing. She give up on Betty and rush back here. Very cross cross! Must hurry!'

'What about Betty?' asked Mrs Bold.

'No know, no see,' she said.

'Right. We thought we were just coming to rescue Bobby. But all of you dogs need to get off this boat, right?'

'Yes please! Don't leave us here with Dog-Mad Debby!' chorused the other dogs. 'We don't want to end up looking like *him*,' they said, nodding towards Bobby.

'Wouldn't dream of it,' Mr McNumpty reassured them.

'Let's get everyone off the boat and onto the dolphins, quick sharp!' said Mr Bold. 'It's going to be a bit crowded but we'll manage somehow.'

'Hurry!' cried Minnie. 'There isn't a moment to lose!'

Everyone rushed up the stairs followed by the Afghan hound (who was really Trumpy, who was really Bobby, who was really a hyena) and the five other dogs. Across the water, halfway back from the rock, they could see Dog-Mad Debby in her inflatable dinghy rowing directly towards them.

Miranda whistled to the dolphins who all bobbed about at the stern of the boat by the ladder, ready for their passengers.

'Er, the thing is,' Mr Bold explained to the dolphins, 'there are another five dogs to be rescued, not just Bobby. Can you manage us all?'

Galileo answered doubtfully: 'Well, I'm not sure we can carry you all. And there are a number of health and safety regulations which I fear may be breached.'

'Can you please try?' asked Mr Bold desperately.

But their conversation was suddenly interrupted. Debby had turned her head when she heard Miranda's shrill whistle. 'Oi!' she shouted gruffly. 'Who's on my boat? Gerroff NOW!' And she began to row much faster. 'I'll get ya!' she yelled. 'Who are ya? Pesky pirates?'

'Quick, everyone pick up a dog each,' instructed Mr Bold, 'and let's get out of here as fast as we can.'

The ladder down to the water was very

narrow and only one person at a time could descend. Uncle Tony went first, but he was elderly and clutching a cockapoo under one arm, which meant he only had one hand to hold onto the ladder, so it was slow progress. When he finally reached the bottom he gingerly placed one foot on a dolphin's back, before stepping off with the other. He then crouched down while holding onto the bewildered dog and gripped hold of the fin on the dolphin's back.

'Right. I've done it,' he said shakily and the dolphin swam steadily off with the heavy load on his back, and the next dolphin took her place by the ladder.

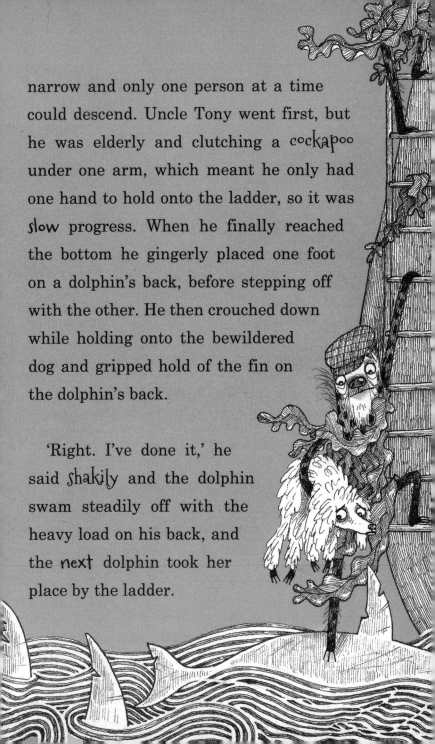

Galileo, who was swimming around directing the proceedings from the water, popped his head up. 'Could I just point out that time is of the essence here? If we all take as long as Uncle Tony just has, that rather unsavoury woman will have time to get back on board and make herself a cheesy omelette before you are all safely disembarked.'

Galileo was right. Debby was only about twenty metres away now, splashing furiously and still yelling threats and insults.

Next in line was Mrs Bold, carrying a panting King Charles spaniel. Amelia transferred herself to her dolphin and was off, but there was still Mr Bold, Minnie, Mr McNumpty and Miranda to go, not to mention Bobby and three other dogs – and Dog-Mad Debby was almost upon them.

'We're not going to make it in time!' cried Minnie.

I'm afraid it was true. Debby had now reached the boat and was waving an oar in the air, trying to swipe at Mr Bold who was attempting to get to the stairs with a Jack Russell under his arm.

'I'll get you! Rob me of my dogs, will you? We'll see about that!' She was red in the face, and if she had her way, would do the intruders some serious harm with the wooden oar she was swinging about.

'This is quite an oar-deal,' said Mr Bold.

Galileo, who together with the other dolphins had retreated a few metres out of Debby's range, called out: 'Only solution – you'll all have to run to the bow of the boat and jump in the water! We'll convene with you there. But I'm not even sure we will be able to carry you all.'

'Right-o!' said Mr Bold. 'Do your best. Everyone hear that? Come on, quick as you can. Up to the front. We're going to have to jump overboard.'

'Yikes!' said Miranda.

'We can do it,' said Mr Bold. 'But we'll have to be quick.'

Everyone ran to the bow of the boat and peered over the side into the gloomy water below.

'Quick! Jump!' said Mr Bold.

'Ready when you are, chaps!' called Galileo.

'I'd get a wiggle on if I were you. Debby is halfway up the ladder now.'

'But we must get the other dogs too!' cried Minnie desperately. The dogs were bewildered by all the frantic activity and getting hold of them again took time. Time they didn't have.

Finally Minnie got hold of Walter and climbed on the rail with Miranda clinging to her arm.

'Me hold your nose,' Miranda offered kindly, and her little monkey fingers held Minnie's nostrils firmly shut.

'On the count of three!' said Mr Bold. 'One, two, three!'

Minnie leaped forward and a second later there was a loud *splash* as she landed in the sea. By the time she reached the surface, Galileo had slid expertly underneath her and he, Minnie, Walter and Miranda were on their way back to shore.

This left Mr McNumpty, Mr Bold and Bobby on the deck, clutching the last two remaining dogs – the Jack Russell and a black Labrador-cross-setter. But it was too late. Just as they were about to follow Minnie over the side of the boat there was a loud, angry grunt behind them. Dog-Mad Debby had made it on to the deck, and with a deep, rasping breath she charged towards them, the wooden oar aimed firmly at their heads.

Suddenly, out of desperation, instinct took over Mr McNumpty, Bobby and Mr Bold – and transformed them. What sort of instinct do you think it was? That's correct. ANIMAL instinct! They put the dogs they were carrying down and what Dog-Mad Debby saw next stopped her in her tracks.

Mr Bold was on all fours, his head lowered, eyes flashing, teeth bared. Bobby was a mini version of his father. They charged towards Dog-Mad Debby, a fierce hunting cry piercing the air. Then Mr McNumpty suddenly seemed twice as tall, his arms raised above his head as he bellowed in full grizzly fashion.

Within a second the three animals had overpowered the now terrified Debby. Mr McNumpty held her in a vice-like bear hug, Mr Bold looked as if he were about to sink his fangs into her and Bobby sniffed at her, then pulled a disgusted face.

'Yuck!' he said.

'Gotcha!' growled Nigel McNumpty.

'Let me go! You animals!' hissed Debby, struggling to get free.

'Shall we tie her up and then jump onto the dolphins?' asked Bobby, peering over the side of the boat.

'Er, problemo!' said Galileo. 'Three dolphins have set off for the shore, fully loaded up and I've sent another to collect young Betty.

Only me and my friend Socrates left, I'm afraid, and we can't manage all three of you and the dogs. Only solution I can come up with is you stay on board. Dump Dog-Mad Debby on the rock and then sail the boat to the beach. We'll all meet there.'

'We've never piloted a boat before!' said Mr McNumpty. 'We are a couple of hyenas and a bear, remember.'

'Piece of cake, old chap!' said Galileo. 'You don't have to sail it anyway; there's an engine. Just pull up the anchor, start the engine and aim for the shore. What could possibly go wrong?'

To begin with everything went smoothly. While Bobby guarded Debby, growling and snapping at her every time she so much as twitched, Mr McNumpty and Mr Bold managed to raise the anchor and then steer the boat to the rock. They had rather enjoyed behaving wildly and ferociously again and as soon as the boat reached the rock, a terrified Debby leaped off it, swimming the last few metres to safety, and sat huddled alone as far from them as possible while the animals set sail for the shore.

'Good riddance!' shouted Bobby.

What lies at the bottom of the ocean and quivers?

A nervous wreck!

Finally, all the drama of Bobby's rescue seemed to be over.

'Thanks, Dad. Thanks, Mr McNumpty,' said Bobby with a sigh. 'I always knew you'd come to save me.'

'No problem, son!' said Mr Bold. 'We missed you so much. Your poor mother was beside herself.'

'And I missed her, and you and Betty and everyone as well. I even missed your terrible jokes!'

'In that case,' said Mr Bold eagerly, 'you'll be wanting to hear some more as soon as possible . . .'

Everyone groaned.

Fred, Bobby and Mr McNumpty were now laughing so much they didn't realise how close they were to the shore. It was only when Galileo leaped out of the water alongside them and shouted, 'Land ahoy, chaps!' that they noticed.

'Oops!' said Mr McNumpty.

'Where are the brakes on this thing?' asked Mr Bold.

But it was too late. With a sickening crunch the boat ran aground. There was a loud creak and it slowly lolloped over onto one side.

Bobby looked down at his feet and saw water seeping through the planks. 'Oh no, Dad!' he said. 'You've wrecked the boat!'

'Abandon ship!' said Mr Bold. But as they

were already on the beach, it only took a couple of leaps and finally Fred, Mr McNumpty, Bobby and the two rescued dogs were safely on dry land again.

'I might have wrecked the boat,' said Mr Bold, 'but at least that means an end to Debby's dog-napping activities, if ever she gets off that rock.'

'Every cloud has a silver lining,' chuckled Mr McNumpty, giving his pal a manly hug.

Chapter

Betty had been delivered to the beach ahead of the others. She thanked her dolphin very much, wrapped herself in a towel and paced up and down, peering out towards the horizon and feeling decidedly anxious and lonely. She wanted, more than anything, to see her twin brother Bobby again. He was annoying sometimes, but she had missed him terribly and she wanted him home safely.

When the boat crashed she held her breath but then leaped with joy when she saw everyone step safely ashore.

'Bobby!' she called, splashing into the waves to greet him.

'Betty!' cried her brother, and the twins hugged each other, rolling around on the sand and chasing about, greeting each other in what I can only describe as true, natural hyena fashion.

Everyone was thrilled to be back on dry land. They all gave three hearty cheers to Galileo and the school of dolphins.

Mr Bold thought it appropriate to make a speech. 'Ahem! Dear dolphins, one and all – you have been a vital part of tonight's rescue, as has Pamela the puffing puffin, and we can't thank you all enough. If it hadn't been for your help, these dogs would have had a very grim future and we, as a family, would have spent the rest of our days searching for Bobby. How can we ever thank you?'

'Well, thank you too, for all you do for animals everywhere,' called Galileo from the shallow water where he and his dolphin friends were listening attentively. 'No acts of kindness go unnoticed, I'm here to tell you. We animals must all stick together. It's the only way to get things done. You know that. We dolphins know that. Deep down, everyone knows it. Even humans!

'And the second most important thing in

the world, after kindness, is to HAVE FUN! So tell us another of your highly amusing jokes, please!'

'Very well!' said Mr Bold. 'How about a limerick this time, as it's a special occasion?'

The dolphins all clapped their enthusiasm. (In the Christmas cracker industry, limericks are reserved for the most expensive, top-of-the-range crackers.)

'Very well, here goes!'

There once was a man from Peru
Who dreamed that he swallowed his shoe.
He woke up in fright
In the midst of the night
To learn that his dream had come true!

The limerick went down very well, and after the applause stopped another was asked for.

A mouse in her room woke Miss Dowd
She was frightened – it must be allowed.
Soon a happy thought hit her –
To scare off the critter,
She sat up in bed and meowed!

'One more, please!' begged Galileo appreciatively.

'More! More! More!' chorused the other dolphins.

'Er, we ought to get going,' interjected Mrs Bold. 'Everyone's rather cold, and Walter's teeth are chattering. We must get back to the tent and dry ourselves off.'

'Quite right,' said Mr Bold. 'And we'd better leave before any questions are asked about what remains of Debby's boat.'

'And I'll phone the Coastguard and say that I think I spotted a woman sitting on a rock out at sea,' said Mrs Bold.

'But, Mum, she doesn't deserve rescuing,' argued Betty. 'She dog-napped Bobby, don't forget!'

'Evil and crazy as she is, we wouldn't want her to die of pneumonia, would we?' reasoned her mother. 'We animals are not as cruel as humans, Betty. Please don't forget that.'

'Just one last limerick, then we had better say our goodbyes,' said Mr Bold.

285

> There was an old man with a beard
> Who said, 'It's just as I feared!
> Two owls and a hen
> Four larks and a wren
> Are making a nest in my beard.'

Everyone thanked the dolphins again, who then did a **spectacular** leaping, spinning and diving display as they swam back out to sea.

At last the Bolds and the rescued dogs piled into the Honda – a dripping, steaming, tired carload – and soon they were back in the tent at Sunnyside Campsite. It was rather late, and by the time everyone had changed out of their wet clothes and the dogs had all been given a good rub down with towels, they realised how **hungry** they all were.

'I don't have much dog food, I'm afraid,' said

Mrs Bold, looking in the food box. 'In fact, I don't have any. And the shop isn't open now. I'm going to have to improvise with what I've got. Then we'll all share it. Who knows what it will taste like . . . Now let me see . . .'

Mrs Bold got a big bowl, into which she put everything she could find:

Two tins of baked beans
Six eggs
A bar of chocolate
Half a loaf of sliced bread
A litre of semi-skimmed milk
A dozen cooked sausages
Some strawberries
A bag of Brussels sprouts (uncooked)
A packet of biscuits
Three big packets of prawn cocktail crisps
A bottle of tomato ketchup
A jar of peanut butter
Half a bottle of lemonade

She then mixed it all up and simmered it in a saucepan on a low heat for twenty minutes. She tasted it, thought for a moment, then added some salt and pepper. The taste is difficult to describe, even for a talented writer like myself. Let's just say it was unusual.

'A sensation!' declared Amelia. 'I don't have enough plates or bowls, I'm afraid,' she said to all the hungry faces looking up at her, 'so I'll just put it in a bowl down on the floor in the middle and we can all dive in. Animal fashion.'

It's just as well it was late and all their camping neighbours were asleep, because it was a rather vulgar sight.

'What is it, exactly?' asked Minnie, looking doubtfully at the pinky brown slop that was spilling over the side of the bowl.

'Um. Well,' said Mrs Bold. 'It's, er, a Cornish recipe I've just invented. Let's call it the Chef's Surprise.'

'It'll be a surprise if we can eat it!' muttered Mr McNumpty.

But everyone was so hungry they soon got stuck in, taking turns to slurp up the concoction (apart from Minnie who, being the only human there, insisted on using a spoon.)

'Delicious!' declared Uncle Tony, licking his lips.

'Is there any more?' asked Bobby.

'I'm afraid that's the lot,' said Mrs Bold. 'Although I have got some mints if anyone needs something to freshen the palate?'

But after such an adventurous, dramatic night, everyone was exhausted, and the sudden need to sleep was quite overpowering.

'In the morning we'll sort out getting you dogs back to your owners,' announced Mr Bold, as everyone started to yawn. 'But for now, well, we'll all have to sleep in the tent wherever we can find a space.'

Several of the dogs were already fast asleep by now, curled up right where they'd been sitting. The bigger dogs slept just outside the tent – on guard, just in case Dog-Mad Debby managed to track them down. And little Walter found a cosy spot inside Minnie's sleeping bag with her.

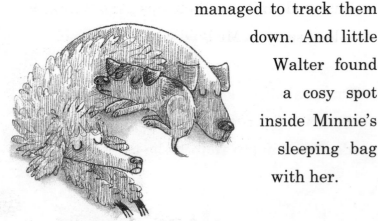

As everyone settled down Mr Bold managed just one goodnight joke.

What did the big candle say to the little candle?

I'm going out tonight!

His audience was too tired to laugh, he told himself, but everyone fell asleep with a contented smile on their lips. And within a couple of seconds Mr Bold was snoring too.

Chapter

22

The next morning some of the dogs woke up with a stomach ache, for which they blamed last night's Chef's Surprise. In fact, there were several emergency dashes to the sand dunes . . .

The shop was open so a more conventional breakfast was bought and eaten; then Mr Bold took out a paper and pen and asked each of the rescued dogs where they lived.

'Forty-one Fairfield Road, Teddington!' said Bobby.

'Yes, dear, we know where you live,' said Mrs Bold. 'But what about the others? Walter?'

Walter was still sleepy, and peeped his snout out from Minnie's jumper. 'I don't know if I can remember,' he said vaguely. 'It's been a week since Debby stole me. I was asleep in my owner's handbag on the beach,' he recalled. 'Then she lifted me up, and put me in a big sack. Oh, it was horrible. Horrible!' He retreated back inside the jumper.

'Well, can you describe the house you lived in?' coaxed Betty.

'It had a roof,' offered Walter. 'And a door and windows, I seem to remember . . . I wasn't very happy there.'

'Very helpful,' sighed Mr McNumpty. 'Next?'

'I know where I live,' said the black Labrador-cross-setter confidently. (He had been painted white with black spots by Dog-mad Debby in order to be sold as another Dalmatian – now most of the paint had come off in the sea, and the rest when he'd been rubbed down with a towel.) 'In Camomile cottage, twenty miles away.'

'Well, if you give me the directions I'll take you there in the car,' said Mr Bold.

'Oh no, my dear Mr Bold,' said the Labrador-cross-setter. 'I think maybe you've been living as a human for a little too long. I don't need a car and directions to get home.' He sniffed the air. 'I'm a *dog*, and I have a very good sense of smell. I've been cooped up on that boat for days – there's nothing I'd like more than a good run all the way home! Thank you so much for everything. Good luck, everyone!'

And with that he bounded off down the beach in the direction of Carbis Bay.

The (rather portly) King Charles spaniel, it turned out, lived very close to the campsite, with a retired couple called Ursula and Derek. 'They're so very kind,' he said wistfully. 'They'll be very worried about me, I expect. What time is it?'

Mrs Bold consulted her watch. 'Almost ten o'clock,' she said.

'Oh, good. They always give me a digestive biscuit at about half past ten.

Let's hurry.' And he went and stood by the Honda.

'It isn't very far away,' said Mr Bold. 'You could walk there in a few minutes.'

'Not with my hips,' muttered the King Charles. 'If you'd be so kind?'

So Mr Bold gave him a lift home, dropping him at the gate just as Ursula came out to put something in the dustbin. As he waddled up the path towards his elderly owner, she let out a cry of joy. 'Rubens! You've come home!' And she scooped him up and smothered him with kisses.

The cockapoo, Buddy, was also soon reunited

with his owners, who lived nearby too. They had posted notes on all the lampposts about their lost dog, and were absolutely delighted when Uncle Tony knocked on their door with the little dog on a lead. Buddy was so thrilled to be home he immediately cocked his leg on the gatepost, and then ran around in circles in the garden. He was home!

Nellie the Jack Russell, it turned out, didn't live anywhere. She'd been a street dog all her life, stealing scraps here and there and sleeping rough until caught late one night in Debby's net. In fact, of all the dogs, she hadn't really minded life on Debby's boat. 'I mean, really, mate,' she said to Betty, 'roof over me head. Grub provided. What's not to like?'

But then Bobby's friend, Taxi, came to welcome him home, took one look at Nellie, and they fell instantly in love. Just like that. Taxi's owners seemed to like Nellie too, so within a few hours she'd moved into their tent.

She ran back at lunch time to tell the Bolds of her new living arrangements. 'Result!' she said, with a glint in her eye and was off again, hotly pursued by a smitten Taxi.

So then there was just Walter left. He showed no signs of wanting to go anywhere. Minnie had dressed him in one of Miranda's onesies so he didn't get cold, but he was happiest being carried around inside her hoodie all day, peering out at a world he didn't much want to investigate.

'Don't you miss your owner?' Mrs Bold asked him one day.

He shook his head. 'I think I was just an accessory for her,' he said. 'She liked carrying me round in her designer handbags and showing me off to her friends. But when we were at home . . .' He trailed off into silence.

'Didn't she play with you?' asked Amelia.

'No,' he said.

'Did she take you out for a walk?'

Walter shook his head. 'It was like I wasn't there.'

So Walter stayed with the Bolds and became very attached to Minnie, who of course had always wanted a puppy of her own. Slowly, over the last days of their holiday, he became happier and more confident. He even managed a brief paddle in the sea and had a quick run along the beach with Bobby and Betty before scurrying back to Minnie and asking to be picked up.

'Well, I've asked all around, and at the Dogs' Home, and no one has reported little Walter missing, so it looks like he will be coming home to live with *us*,' said Mr Bold.

'I'm fine with that,' said Mrs Bold. 'We've got plenty of room and he's a *dear* little chap. Minnie can come and see him every day then, so it will be almost like having her own dog.'

On the last day of the holiday, Mrs Bold slipped away from the beach to pay a visit to Tiddles Tea Shop on St Ives High Street.

'Ah, Mrs Bold!' said Bertha. 'I hear you found your son. How purrrfectly wonderful!'

'Yes,' beamed Amelia. 'And I wanted to thank you for the information you gave me about Dog-Mad Debby. You were quite right about her.'

'Oh, don't mention it,' said Bertha, bowing her head with modesty. 'We animals are always willing to help each other. Especially where a human as dastardly as Dog-Mad Debby is concerned.'

'She ought to be stopped before she steals any more poor dogs from the street,' said Mrs Bold. 'I've been worrying about that.'

'All done!' said Bertha, flashing the claws of one paw very briefly so Mrs Bold could see. 'I won't bore you with the details, but let's just say Debby won't be bothering any more dogs.'

Amelia gasped. 'Ah! You didn't, you know, hurt her in any way, did you?'

Bertha smiled. 'Ask me no questions and I'll tell you no lies. Now, can I interest you in one of our tasty Cornish pasties?'

Mrs Bold gasped again. 'Bertha, you didn't? You've put Dog-Mad Debby in a pasty?'

'No, of course not!' said Bertha. 'What kind of an establishment do you think this is? No, I've got Debby where I can keep an eye on her. She's poor now that she's lost her boat and her business. Came looking for some work. Wants to go legit now. I think you Bolds have shown her that crime doesn't pay. Well, you know how busy it can get around here in the holiday season . . . so I've given her a job – washing up. She wouldn't dare try any funny business with me. OR I MIGHT TRY A NEW SPAGHETTI BOLOGNAISE RECIPE I'VE HEARD ABOUT,' she shouted loudly so that anyone in the back kitchen could hear.

Mrs Bold couldn't help but let out a hyena-like cackle. Then she said a fond farewell to Bertha and left the cafe.

Chapter

So the Bolds' holiday finally came to an end.
The tent was taken down and everything was
packed up and loaded in the boot or on the roof
rack and everyone squeezed into the little blue
Honda for the return journey.

'Goodbye, everyone!'
said Pam the puffing
puffin, flying in a farewell
circle around the car. 'Hope
to see you next year! Agas gweles!'

'Thanks for everything, Pam. Look after yourself,' said Mrs Bold. 'We'll definitely be back!'

'What a **splendid** holiday adventure we've all had,' said Mr McNumpty as they began the long journey home.

'No one would believe all the things that have happened!' said Uncle Tony.

'Me loopy loop on surfy board!' squealed Miranda.

'I got dog-napped and taken out to sea!' said Bobby.

'I rode on a dolphin's back!' said Betty.

'I met a **perfect** little dog!' said Minnie.

'Funny how wonderful things happen to us Bolds,' said Fred contentedly. 'Which bit did you like best, Amelia?' he asked his wife.

'Well,' said Mrs Bold with a smile. 'Getting Bobby back was the best bit, of course . . . But our holiday isn't over yet, is it? Maybe the best is yet to come.'

'You don't mean . . .'

'Yes, I do. TELL US SOME JOKES!'

So Mr Bold did. Lots and lots of them. Here are just three, to give you the flavour. (I've picked the best of a motley bunch.)

How do fleas travel?

By itch-hiking!

And so the jokes continued.

On and on until they arrived home in Teddington, happy and helpless with laughter.

P.S.

But guess what? Do you remember the reason Minnie's father wouldn't let her have a dog? I told you way back at the beginning of the book . . .

Correct! Because he was allergic to dog fur.

But what is unusual about Walter?

Yup. He is hairless!

So what do you suppose happened when they got back to Teddington?

That's right too! Minnie was allowed to keep Walter – she got the puppy she had always wanted.

Sigh.

Tears of joy and all that sort of thing.

If this isn't the happiest ending to any book ever written, I'll eat one of Mrs Bold's hats. So there!

MR BOLD'S JOKES

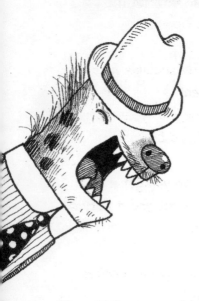

What do you get when you cross a fly, a car and a dog?
A flying carpet!

Did you hear about the race between the lettuce and the tomato?
The lettuce got a 'head' and the tomato was trying to 'ketchup'!

How do fleas travel?
By itch-hiking!

What did one petrol tank say to the other petrol tank?
What do you take me for? A fuel?

How do you make a sausage roll?
Push it downhill!

Doctor, Doctor, I keep thinking I'm a nit.
Will you please get out of my hair!

Doctor, Doctor, I keep thinking I'm a dog.
Sit!

What do dogs eat at the movies?
Pupcorn!

Why do bananas put on sunscreen before they go to the beach?
In case they peel!

Where do pencils go on holiday?
Pencil-vania!

What time should you go to the dentist?
Tooth-hurty!

Did the dolphin break the vase by accident?
No, he did it on porpoise!

What did Cinderella dolphin wear to the ball?
Glass flippers!

Why do seagulls fly over the sea?
Because if they flew over the bay they'd be bagels!

What do you get if you cross a cat and a parrot?
A carrot!

Why are pirates called pirates?
They just arrrrgh!

Doctor, Doctor, I keep thinking I'm a frog.
What's wrong with that?
I'm worried I'm going to croak it!

What do you get if you cross a fish with an elephant?
Swimming trunks!

What happens when a frog's car breaks down?
It gets toad away!

What do you get if you cross a dog with a calculator?
A dog you can count on!

Why did the lobster blush?
Because the sea weed!

What's the difference between a fish and a piano?
You can't tuna fish!

How do fish get to school?
By octobus!

What kind of noise annoys an oyster?
A noisy noise annoys an oyster!

What did the big candle say to the little candle?
I'm going out tonight!

What do you call a dog with no legs?
It doesn't matter what you call him, he still won't come!

What do snakes have embroidered on their bath towels?
Hiss and hers!

Why did the elephant wear pink pyjamas?
Because his blue ones were in the wash!

Why did the golfer wear two pairs of pants?
Because he had a hole in one!

Did you hear about the man who slept with his head under the pillow?
When he woke up he discovered the fairies had taken all his teeth!

A polar bear walks into a fish and chip shop and says, 'I'll have a cup of tea please and . . . . a large cod and chips.'
'Certainly,' says the girl serving him. 'But why the large pause?'
'I dunno,' said the polar bear. 'I've always had those.'

When Julian Clary isn't having a silly time dressing up and telling jokes on stage, he likes to be at home with his pets. He has lots of them: dogs, cats, ducks and chickens. His life-long love of animals inspired him to tell a story about what would happen if they pretended to be like us. Julian also loves touring the country, reading his books aloud to children and animals alike.

David Roberts always loved to draw and paint as a child, and when he grew up his talents took him all the way to Hong Kong where he got a job making beautiful hats. But he always wanted to illustrate children's books, and so he came back to England to work with the finest authors in the land. David loves drawing animals and clothes and hats, so what could be better than a book about animals *in* clothes and hats?